BLACK MENACE

BLACK MENACE: Scourge of an Apocalyptic World
Copyright © 2022 by Kenneth J. Sousa

Published in the United States of America
ISBN   Paperback: 978-1-959165-64-4
ISBN   eBook: 978-1-959165-65-1

All rights reserved. No part of this publication may be reproduced, stored in a retrieval system or transmitted in any way by any means, electronic, mechanical, photocopy, recording or otherwise without the prior permission of the author except as provided by USA copyright law.

The opinions expressed by the author are not necessarily those of ReadersMagnet, LLC.

ReadersMagnet, LLC
10620 Treena Street, Suite 230 | San Diego, California, 92131 USA
1.619. 354. 2643 | www.readersmagnet.com

Book design copyright © 2022 by ReadersMagnet, LLC. All rights reserved.

Cover design by Kent Gabutin
Interior design by Daniel Lopez

BLACK MENACE

SCOURGE OF AN APOCALYPTIC WORLD

By
KENNETH J. SOUSA

ReadersMagnet, LLC

CONTENTS

Chapter One	The Slaughter	1
Chapter Two	The Sage	9
Chapter Three	Greybeard	14
Chapter Four	The Battle of the Dark Marsh	18
Chapter Five	The Spy	28
Chapter Six	Under the Bridge	35
Chapter Seven	Mik Meets Bek	44
Chapter Eight	Zignoid's Report	50
Chapter Nine	Bek	57
Chapter Ten	Mindfulness Comes to the Lake	66
Chapter Eleven	Mik and Bek Mate	76
Chapter Twelve	Starting a Family	83
Chapter Thirteen	Raising Fledglings	89
Chapter Fourteen	Trouble on the Channel	93
Chapter Fifteen	Militia to Army	97
Chapter Sixteen	Unexpected Visitors	103
Chapter Seventeen	Jull	112
Chapter Eighteen	Mik's Marauders	116
Chapter Nineteen	Courageous Mik	128
Chapter Twenty	Mik Takes Command	133
Chapter Twenty One	Return to Island	140
Chapter Twenty Two	The Plan	151

Chapter Twenty Three	The West Army	156
Chapter Twenty Four	The Defense	160
Chapter Twenty Five	The War	166
Chapter Twenty Six	Aftermath	178
Chapter Twenty Seven	Return of the Sage	182
Chapter Twenty Eight	Black Menace	188
Chapter Twenty Nine	Ending the Menace	193
Chapter Thirty	Another Season	198
Epilogue		198

ONE
THE SLAUGHTER

Excitement reigned in the *moorhen* nest, even before the sun came up. Today was the day the six young fledglings would be led out to the open lake for the first time. Although the fledglings were hungry, they kept their peeps to a minimum; that is except for Mik, who still slept in his usual dark spot. It then took all of his five siblings to shake him awake. This scene was not uncommon. Mik had been the last egg in the brood to hatch and was always the hatchling who gave his parents trouble. He was the runt of the brood and early on had earned the nickname, Mischief.

It was just at sunrise when their father, Flik and mother, Luun, got their brood into single file and led them into the reeds surrounding their nest on the shore of a long Florida lake. They had been taught from a young age to travel in single file and of course Mik was always last. Their small slender bodies let them easily slip through the thick reeds. Flik had already taken a cautious look at the open lake through the last row of reeds when Mik spied a bush holding a branch of ripe berries back in the nest's direction. The incorrigible runt couldn't help himself. He just had to go back and try a mouthful of those delicious looking fruit.

By the time Mik had eaten his fill, he realized he had fallen far behind his family and rushed to catch up. When Mischief finally emerged from the reeds, the first thing he witnessed was an enormous alligator stalking his family. Before he could squawk a weak *kuuuk* of warning, the alligator smashed the birds with his tail and devoured the entire group. Mik, stunned, froze in place at the devastating sight. His only movement was the dipping of his body caused by the ripples as the alligator disappeared into the depths of the cloudy water.

After a time, nature intervened to change Mik's shock to fear in order for him to escape the same fate as his family. Self preservation forced his long scrawny legs to push his thin body deep into the tangled reeds until his feet touched the bottom of the lake shore. He finally stopped to weep for his terrible loss and an abrupt realization of being completely alone on the large dangerous lake.

It wasn't until near starvation drove him to seek food that at last he was able to prod himself to move again. Being close to the shoreline, Mik stepped up on hard ground and was further from the ferocious alligator. As he pecked at the ground for tender shoots of new grass and an occasional insect, he speculated on what else the lake had in store for him, especially as a small young moorhen whose soft pink beak had yet to turn red and hard for defense. To Mik, the only form of defense he could imagine was his own wits.

Mik was a *moorhen*, a duck-like bird scientifically called *Gallinule Chloropus* or *Common Moorhen* belonging to the *Rallidae*, also known as the family of *Rail*. Moorhens aren't much larger than an average pigeon and mate for life. Their color is mostly black with a few white tail and wing tip feathers they lift to warn off enemies. The tip of their beak is yellow, but most of the beak is hard, a vivid red and reaches almost to the top of their head, an area called the *shield*, which is their main defense. Moorhens have long yellow legs with no webbing between their clawed toes and when they swim; their long legs force their heads to bob from front to back.

Time passed slowly for Mik in the days after the slaughter. He tried to regain his old nest and territory but was rebuked by a family of squatters who had already taken it over. Mik's beak was still pink and his wits advised him that he had no chance against an adult moorhen with a family. He had no choice but to move on and keep quiet while hiding in the deep reeds.

As time passed, the sun began to grow higher in the sky, Mik's beak grew slightly redder, but for the young moorhen, life had not grown any easier. Luckily, due to his light weight and large feet, he was able to walk on lily pads in order to snatch unwary insects to eat; his parents had already taught him how to dive headfirst in shallow water to find snails and young tender reed shoots. He still grieved for his family which caused his heart to grow harder. He distanced himself from any other bird he might call a friend. Moorhens are naturally cautious, however even with his heightened sense of his surroundings; he still wished to catch a glimpse of Flik or Luun, or possibly sibling who might have escaped the alligator. After a while, it seemed to Mik that even time couldn't heal his loss and as moons passed, his mood and tendency towards violence grew worse.

Problems arose from the fact that other single male moorhens controlled most of the territory surrounding Mik's birth nest. Being extremely territorial, the other moorhens wouldn't let him feed in one place long enough to settle his own territory. This situation caused many clashes between other moorhens and him. Being young and especially small, he lost all his early clashes; thus the more he was shunned the more his heart hardened and his self-esteem lowered. The more his self-esteem lowered, the more Mik's outer self became hard-edged and he outwardly appeared over confidant and aggressive.

In those early skirmishes Mik had been too young to put up much of a fight. However, as he began to age his beak and shield grew redder, along with the anger and frustration with his loss and loneliness. Soon he was winning some territorial battles but he still had not yet found himself a permanent home. Nevertheless he did finally find himself a friend.

One day as he had been pecking for food at the edge of the lake, he was surprised to see two huge birds along with two much smaller birds he assumed were their fledglings; though he had to admit that the fledglings were much larger than him. Under normal circumstances the naturally nervous moorhen would have hurried for safer ground or swam out onto the lake, but this time he felt an unusual affinity for the birds and waited as they approached.

The largest of the birds walked straight to Mik who stood in a cocky pose and was ready to flash his few whitening tail feathers as a warning. The long necked and long legged brown colored bird with small patches of white feathers towered over Mik. Finally in a low pitched accented voice he said,"kuuuk". To Mik the word from the big bird's beak sounded familiar and he understood what it meant. Mik returned the greeting with a squeaky kuuuk, but in front of the brown giant he still held his swaggering position.

The huge bird continued in his deep bass voice. "My name is Coal. I am of the *limpkin* clan and this is my family." Coal swept his large wing towards his family. "This is Shyul, my mate, and my two fledglings are Duug and Kuun."

Mik was still surprised that the younger birds were only fledglings. They both rose to well over his head but he held his impetuous pose and answered Coal. "My name is Mik. I am from the clan they call *moorhen* from the family of *Rail*." As he spoke, Mik struggled to deepen his own voice but he didn't have the size or long neck that his kuuuk's would have needed.

Coal kuuuked without delay, "I know of your clan and of the family of *Rail*. We are cousins from eons back in time as the limpkins were once in the family of *Rail*. We all are blessed to meet you, Mik of the moorhens." The huge bird continued in a gravelly voice but in an accent Mik had been able to understand. Coal spoke frankly to Mik. "You are rather young to be traveling alone, little one. Is your family close by?"

Mik answered somewhat truthfully but his voice still carried the arrogance of overconfidence he used to hide his low self-esteem. "I am *alone* and content with it. My family was slain by the largest, meanest alligator on the lake. I, unaided, survived. So you can plainly see that I can watch out for myself," he pompously expressed to the giant limpkin.

Coal ignored the arrogant tone of the young moorhen's answer and in a voice filled with sympathy he kuuuked, "I have heard from others on the lake of this terrible tragedy. I and my family can say we understand the great grief you must feel. If there is anything we can do, just ask."

Inside his breast Mik's heart was moved by the kind words spoken by the big limpkin, but on the outside he held his cold, egotistical stance and answered, "I do thank you and yours for your kind words, Coal, but I need no help from any bird." Without so much as a goodbye, Mik turned and marched straight for the lake.

Before he reached the water, Coal called out to Mik once again. With no hint of resentment at being insulted by the young moorhen, the limpkin said, "A warning to you then, little Mik. I see you are traveling north and I must warn you. There is a sinister feeling around a dark marsh in your path. It would be wise of you to avoid it at all costs. I no longer can advise you where the marsh begins for it seems a menacing force causes it to grow ever larger with each full moon. I think its intent is to devour all living entities that dwell on or around the lake. The reason for this destruction is known only by the vile spirit behind it. Listen harder to me little moorhen. On your journey, please take a more cautious route."

Acting the pigheaded Mischief, Mik let Coal's cautious words slip past his ears as he moved yet faster bearing north. Swiftly skipping from lily pad to lily pad, Mik's agile beak shoveled in any insect that crossed his path. He thought about his meeting with Coal and remembered his words of kindness. Maybe he was not as alone on the lake as he believed; at least it was comforting to believe so.

After a great deal of traveling, the young moorhen noted that the lily pads he was stepping on were becoming a darker shade of green. Before long he saw that there were no more insects and the pads were completely black. Suddenly, he remembered the warning of Coal and stopped.

Only moments ago he had been traveling in bright sunlight. Now he thought a storm must be coming due to the sudden chill in the air and the dark clouds which filled the sky all the way to the marshy end of the lake. Something about those clouds bothered Mik. To him, they appeared to hang extremely low and were intensely dark. He knew that rain should be falling from them but none came. Next, he noticed the area surrounding him. Everything he saw was rotting. Even the trees surrounding this part of the lake had lost their leaves. The bark on the trees had been stripped to bare black wood and the branches sagged like drooping dead bodies.

Mik observed the thick black pitch-like water surrounding him. The lily pads were also black as death, along with all of the reeds. Finally, to his horror, he noted that mixed in with the mysterious black morass were the bones of many birds. Some were only wing bones but others were whole skeletons, some large, some medium, and some as small as himself. It was hard for him to accept that which was strewn hither and yon in front of him. The only thing his young mind could relate the scene too was the destruction of his own family.

When the memories of his lost family crept into his mind, his first consideration was what event could possibly have caused such a catastrophe. Could it have been alligators, he thought, but he saw no sign of any living creature near this end of the lake. Besides, he considered, if it had been alligators, in the black quagmire there would be no bones left. It must have been caused by something of which he knew nothing.

Unexpectedly, he felt movement in the black marsh under the lily pad his feet stood on. The action almost encompassed the size of the dark section of the lake and seemed to Mik like the thick black morass was taking a deep breath. When the motion subsided, he believed he heard a low murmur. Mik was amazed when out of the pitch- black muck slowly oozed a huge bubble the color of the surrounding sky. As Mik watched in astonishment, the bubble grew in size to where he believed it was about to lift into the air. Abruptly, the bubble burst in all directions and black bone-filled muck reached all the way to the lily pad on which Mik stood, directly followed by a wave of stench which almost knocked him into the muck. To the young moorhen the mess at his feet, along with the putrid smell, felt like a warning. It took only an instant to remember the words of Coal and he realized how unwise it was for him to be standing on a black lily pad in the middle of this horrifyingly evil dark place. Instinctively, he turned, leapt to the dark lily pad behind him and then to another, until there was no mucky water below. He then quickly lunged into clearer water and pushed his still growing legs as fast as possible in the direction where he could see sun shining.

TWO
THE SAGE

Mik bobbed hurriedly down the lake until he found unblackened reeds. Quickly he scrambled into the protection of the green cover. In his hurry to leave the gruesome black sight behind, he failed to see the squinty eyes of a hungry snapping turtle nicknamed, Ol' Mo. The snapper waited patiently for the young moorhen to pass close enough for his long neck to stretch and grasp the unsuspecting bird in his vicious jaws. Suddenly, Mik's nervous senses caught sight of his natural enemy, but as with the fairly recent tragedy of his diseased family, fright took over and he froze in place. As Mik was about to become Ol' Mo's lunch, an equally frightening experience occurred. He suddenly felt the grasp of giant claws seize his tiny body as he was pulled from Ol' Mo's closing jaws. Moorhens can only fly in short low flights, but he now found himself looking down at treetops from high in the sky. Mik was sure his life would end, but instead the ground slowly grew closer and he was deposited gently on the lake shore.

Relieved to discover himself standing safely on solid ground, Mik also found himself staring at large yellow clawed feet. The feet led up to incredibly long yellow legs, which followed up to a huge white feathered body. Mik had to step back from the body to track an extensive neck up to a head with a long, thin pointed beak and a pair of huge eyes looking directly into his. Mik thought the eyes could only belong to one bird on the lake, a massive creature of which he had only heard whispered rumors, a *great white heron*.

The giant white bird spoke to Mik in a loud rumbling voice. "I be called the Sage, an old friend of thy family. From the air I witnessed the horrific end of thy loved ones. To all of our misfortune I be at a distance too great to give any assistance. But to my joy, I be able to rescue thee from thy near demise in the jaws of Ol' Mo. I saved you from the vicious long-necked beast because I owe a debt of honor to Shuul and Buurr, thy grandparents."

The Sage's speech held a regal tone as he told Mik he would become his mentor. To the hard edged cocky young moorhen it did not seem that the huge bird was asking; more like commanding that he was his mentor. Mik felt resentment. His ire rose, but on second thought he realized the big old bird had saved his life and quickly calmed down.

In his bombastic voice, the Sage also explained that Mik would go through a long period of suffering due to the trauma he had experienced: rage, depression, isolation, flashbacks of the incident, guilt, and possibly violence. "These circumstances do not have to last thee a lifetime. There be ways of mending such injuries. But of that I shall teach thee when thou be ready."

The Sage also told of other dangers on the lake besides alligators, such as creatures similar to Ol' Mo who could easily pull a duck or moorhen under water to be eaten, alive or dead. There were snakes and other preying birds, but most dangerous of all for the little moorhen was the great blue heron known as *Greybeard*. Greybeard held sway over what he called his minions, a flock of large ugly ducks called *muscovy*. The minions would carry out every evil desire of Greybeard, which generally led to corralling smaller prey into the ever-ravenous beak of the vile heron. He also told Mik that Greybeard's reputation had flourished due to an extra large row of grey feathers which had suddenly appeared on his breast allowing him to live up to his given name, *Greybeard*. There were some who even believed that the extra beard-like feathers also gave him magical powers.

The Sage said he hated Greybeard and was ashamed to admit that they were related. He and Greybeard were cousins, one white, the other blue and both in the family of *Rail*. In their youth they played as brothers, until one day as they flew across the lake they spied a nest of sparrow fledglings with beaks open, awaiting their parents for feeding. Without a moment's notice Greybeard swept out of the sky and landed on a branch next to the tiny birds. In seconds he had devoured every chick and flown off to rejoin the Sage. The Sage said nothing to his cousin about his disgusting behavior; that was until they had found an old iguana close to death. The Sage wanted to help the old lizard to shade where he could have a restful passing. Greybeard said no, as he shoved the Sage aside in order to lift the dying iguana by the head with his enormous beak and swallow him, even though the lizard's size choked him; this was after Greybeard had eaten a whole nest of fledgling sparrows.

It was at this point that the Sage realized the great evil in his once beloved cousin. In response to Greybeard's actions toward the helpless sparrows and lizard, the Sage moved his breeding territory far from his relative. He moved south past the *Wide Bridge* which divided the long lake. The Sage vowed to himself never to kuuuk hello to the appalling Greybeard again.

"Me thinks enough has been kuuuked of, little one. Just remember, a bird in the sky doth watch over thou. One more thing I be kuuuking, young moorhen. There be sanctuary with many moorhen females on the south side of the Wide Bridge. It be the place thee belong."

Mik had yet to see any bridge on the lake. Immediately he quizzed the Sage about it.

The Sage answered. "There be such a bridge on the lake, some distance to the south. It be of an ancient age; built long before any birds can remember. I have flown over it many times. There be no path leading to either side of the old stone structure, but it be wide with deep dark water below. The only creatures I be aware of using it be a family of *boat-tailed grackles* who nest on its rubble-strewn top and I have had rare views of large bats flying from its deep black innards. Don't worry about it now little one. Thou have much time to grow before thee must pass into its darkness and see for thyself."

Then with a sweep of his great wings Mik watched him lift towards the clouds. As the Sage flew away, Mik wondered why the old bird hated this Greybeard so much. To the brash young moorhen it didn't seem like eating a few young chicks and a dying lizard was enough to dredge up the intense hatred he felt emanating from the great white. Mik hoped that someday he might hear the full story of the trouble with their relationship.

THREE
GREYBEARD

Unbeknown to the two birds conversing on the shore, gliding silently high in the air was the *great blue heron*, Greybeard. Even at great height he could not help but recognize the size and regal bearing of his cousin, the one he most loathed, Sage. As for the other bird whose small stature barely allowed for a decent sighting from such a distance, he guessed he could only be that of a young moorhen; an ancient cousin who split from the Rail family many years before birds were really birds. Why else, he deliberated to himself, would a nervous moorhen stand so close to a great white heron. He considered deeper and remembered the moorhens who he had already encountered; they who had disrupted his plans for the future. He hoped this moorhen did not belong to the same clan. It was his narcissistic belief that he could not possibly have missed killing all of both clans which had so devastated his greatest vision; the takeover of the entire lake. No matter, he contemplated. To make sure, I shall send Goff and his winged hooligans to rid the lake of the tiny pest.

As Greybeard winged back to his hidden lair, he reflected back to when all the changes had occurred. It had been the period just before he and his cousin, Sage, had ceased to be the best of friends.

Even with the large number of seasons which had passed, he could still recall the day he had first discovered the *Dark Marsh*. He had been wading along the north end of the lake seeking a fresh site to wait patiently for a fish to pass before his sharp, quick beak. No fish appeared to choose to be his dinner. Hoping for better luck, he waded a little further north. Suddenly he realized the sun wasn't shining and a chill filled the air. Standing in the water near the shore, he noticed that the water and the banks of the marsh were darker and a large murky cloud covered the area. He thought little of it until he waded into the mysterious looking water of the marsh. Almost instantly he spotted a fairly large fish wriggling along the shore of the lake; one who could possibly be dying. An easy catch he thought until he noticed its color, which would normally be bright silver but had turned to dark grey. He wondered about the safety of eating a dying fish but his hunger got the best of him. He speared the fish and flipped it head first to allow it to slip down his gullet without its fins scratching his throat.

He remembered how odd his stomach felt and had hoped he had not eaten something that would make him sick. He had tried to choke out the dying fish but its fins would not allow it back up his long throat. The longer he choked, the fuzzier his head had begun to feel. He had worried he might pass out and be eaten by an alligator, or perhaps he could possibly be dying himself. Suddenly, he lost consciousness but he slowly reawakened. He recalled that he had passed out on the edge of the lake but could not recall how long he had laid half in and half out of the water. When his senses finally completely returned, he stood quickly on his long wobbly legs. He recollected that at the time he felt he would go mad if he did not fill his stomach with some kind of food. Strangely, a whole school of the half dying grey fish had wriggled before him and he almost drowned gathering and swallowing all he could put down, yet the ravishing hunger had not disappeared.

He was surprised when he had realized his hunger had not dissipated. He was completely aghast that a new set of grey feathers had grown over most of the blue feathers on his chest. He had had no idea of the reason but they had materialized like he had grown an actual grey beard; like he had actually grown into his name.

When Greybeard's mind finally adjusted to his new beard, he realized that ravishing hunger still filled his abdomen. Still more wriggling grey fish appeared at his feet and he ate until he had lost consciousness again.

When he realized he was again in an awakened state, he dragged himself back to his feet. He was still hungry but a new sensation appeared. His mind was not as it had been. He felt that a new world had opened up to him and new ideas passed like a flock of sparrows flying in circles. Suddenly, his mind slowed and the first idea he was able to grasp from the sparrows swirling in his head was to conquer all of the lake in order to never lack for food.

Hunger still ravished his innards but no more grey fish wriggled before him. His only choice was to wade along the lake for another fish to swim by. He was only a short distance from the dark marsh when he spied his cousin, Sage, winging past high in the sky. Greybeard swiftly unfurled his wings and lifted to join his white cousin.

FOUR

THE BATTLE OF THE DARK MARSH

As time progressed the young moorhen, Mik, forgot the close encounter with Ol' Mo, but flashes of the horrible demise of his family crept in and out of his mind's eye. He constantly felt the grief and loss; the need to prove himself to all, the anger, the nervousness and anxiety. Most of all he felt his near total loneliness. Mik couldn't help but believe he might yet find a live parent or sibling in the future to help fill the grieving hole in his heart

One day as he bobbed along searching for food, Mik maliciously took out some of his frustration on a flock of harmless *mottled ducks*. He chased them in all directions until he felt some of his anger subside. After a rest, he spied a flock of white *Ibis* pecking at the ground beyond the lake shore. For no reason other than to vent his anger, he climbed the bank and in an attacking stance he chased the whole flock into the air.

Feeling somewhat more relieved, he reentered the water and wandered through the reeds to the open lake where he found himself confronted by a band of the biggest, smelliest and ugliest ducks he had ever observed. They were twice the size of any duck he had encountered and their feathers sported many colors. It was their faces that sent shivers of fear through his body. Their faces were extremely hideous. They carried a mass of ugly, many-colored scabs reaching from their large beaks down to their necks. He knew instinctively that they must be Greybeard's muscovy minions of which the Sage had spoken, and it didn't take him long to realize they were attempting to surround him.

Mik thought fast. He had been in many small skirmishes with other birds and knew his hardened red shield could be used as a ram, but there were many muscovy and he could hurt but maybe a few. He thought about flying away, but moorhens, although somewhat larger than a pigeon, did not have the wing capability to fly over the heads of the menacing collection now surrounding him.

Mik couldn't fly but he could fight. He felt he was tough, especially when his life was in danger. The few white feathers built into his tail could be used to scare off some predators but not as many big ugly muscovy as he now faced. The only thing he could do was screw up his courage, pick out the largest of the adversaries and attack. He quickly found himself with his head down and his short wings out as he ran across the water straight into the breast of the biggest and ugliest muscovy. The other ducks seemed shocked that such a small bird could cause their leader, Goff, to let out a painful cry, but the attack didn't dissuade them from the orders given by Greybeard.

As the muscovy moved in for the kill, Mik chose another enemy and charged in his direction. Just as he was about to head-butt the minion, his opponent was suddenly lifted into the air and thrown through the sky. Bewildered by the event, Mik turned to see the Sage grab another muscovy with his enormous beak and toss him aside. At that point the rest of the flock took panicked flight, leaving only torn feathers, ripples, Mik and the Sage.

The Sage looked sternly down at the small black moorhen. Mik felt guilty for needing the Sage's help again, but the little moorhen took a bold stance at having beaten ugly Goff. The Sage ignored the young moorhen's prideful carriage and spoke with an even deeper rumble as he told Mik that he and Greybeard had had many problems down through the seasons and that Greybeard somehow had learned of Mik's existence. Now Greybeard would hear of his survival against his fierce muscovy leader, Goff.

"Me thinks that Greybeard will stop at nothing to destroy thee little moorhen. Now thou must listen to my words, little brave one." The deep voice of the huge great white heron rumbled to Mik's core. "I know thy bloodline and I know of the great courage which flows through thy tiny body. Thou can combat thy fears and travel to the safer side of the Wide Bridge. There be a great extent of territory for thee to locate a mate and nesting ground. Thou be the last of your line of moorhens and it be thy duty to continue it. I cannot come to thy rescue at every turn. The event which just occurred proves that Greybeard knows of thy existence. He will stop at nothing to end thy bloodline. It be now that thee must gather thou courage and travel through the dark waters under the Wide Bridge to a new life that awaits thee."

Mik felt true pride surge through his frame as opposed to the usual low self-esteem he used his false pride to cover. As he listened to what the Sage was telling him he found a new strength within. With that new strength he felt he was ready to ask the great Sage about a problem that was bothering him. "Tell me mighty Sage, why is it that you hate this Greybeard so much?"

The Sage answered gravely. "I feel thou be now old enough to hear the answer to thy question little one. But I must warn thee, the answer will not be pretty. It be a story of deceit, wickedness, spilled blood of many innocents and the evil place known as the *Dark Marsh*."

The horror Mik felt in the marsh filled his mind, but he had to know the story. He recalled the scene the limpkin, Coal, had warned him away from, however he eased himself from his brash stance and listened intently, eager to hear the story the Sage would reveal. "I am young Great One, but I have stood on my own this long spring. I have seen the dark marsh of which you speak. I must hear from you the tale of the great destruction I found there. I am ready to hear your story."

"I have already kuuuked to thee of my parting ways with my immoral cousin, Greybeard. Nevertheless there be much more to the story I be sure will interest thee. As I told thee, after the breakup with my cousin I had traveled to the farthest end of the lake and founded a new territory for myself. It was in this place where my life would make a great change.

In my new territory I believed my life could never be better until one day while flying above another lake I be stopping to rest. It be there that I met the most exquisite female great white heron the eye could behold. Her feathers were as white as the whitest cloud and she carried herself with the regalness of a queen. It be instant love for us both. Her name be *Norce*.

After a long mating ritual we nested together and Norce produced two beautiful greenish blue eggs. As be the custom of the great whites, we both incubated the eggs in turn while making sure we nudged the eggs to the opposing sides of the shell many times per day. Finally, our patience be rewarded when two hatchling whites burst forth from their shells and repeatedly kuuuked for food. At once I took flight in search of a water moccasin to chew and feed our hatchlings.

One day when flying home with dinner for my young ones I noticed a flash of blue in the distance near our nest. Instinctively I knew there be danger. My fearful thoughts immediately turned to Greybeard. I dropped the dead snake dangling from my claws and beat my wings more swiftly to save my family. Just as I be reaching the nest I saw Greybeard swallowing the second of my hatchlings. Making the scene even worse, I witnessed Norce lying dead against the side of our nest; from her heart red blood flowed over her beautiful white feathers. From the size and shape of the wound I knew it be rammed into her by the long bloody beak of mine own cousin, Greybeard.

Greybeard kuuuked at me that Norce hadn't put up much of a fight along with a hideous laugh. Before I could pounce on the revolting

Greybeard, he lifted his great blue wings and flew off, leaving me with only a dead white body and my heart breaking with grief.

In time, my grief subsided enough for me to think clearly. My first reaction be to catch Greybeard and pierce *his* black heart. But on second thought I remembered Greybeard ruled a flock of muscovy ducks near his territory in the *Dark Marsh*. Using a rude sign language, Greybeard had threatened their thick-headed muscovy leader, Goff, with a promise that he would eat all his chicks and annihilate his harem if he refused to do his bidding. To prove his point, Greybeard had quickly snatched a muscovy chick and tossed it down his long throat. That gesture and the fear of losing his harem, and thus his clan leadership, forced Goff to pledge total allegiance to the vile great blue heron.

The muscovy be an ugly flock of large ducks and the males be known to keep a harem of females for their own pleasure. Tis be true that they would even steal another hen from a weaker muscovy to grow their own harem. Most birds kept their distance from the muscovy, not only because of their ugly looks and polygamous ways but also for their foul smell. They be called muscovy because of their heavy musk scent. Of the whole flock, Goff be the largest, ugliest, and the foulest smelling.

Even in my profound state of grief and vast thirst for revenge, I be knowing that alone I be no match against Greybeard and his mob of stinking thugs. I thought hard about who might ally with me against Greybeard. There be few great white herons in the area and no others on this lake. My next thought be of another of my cousins, the limpkins. Limpkins be a little shorter than meself and brown in color, with small patches of white on their bodies. However, my Rail cousins be somewhat stouter then me or Greybeard. I also held knowledge that the limpkins retained a grudge against Greybeard, who for his own sadistic pleasure had killed several of their chicks. I believed they be glad to get some much needed revenge against their tormentor. As an afterthought I be picturing another bird from way back in the Rail family; the pigeon-size black birds with red beaks called, moorhens." The Sage gave a nod of recognition to Mik and continued. "I immediately dismissed that thought as I held that moorhens could not possibly be a match for the likes of the large muscovy or their much larger leader, Greybeard. I be quickly throwing the idea of moorhens aside and decided on seeking out the limpkins.

I knew the limpkin clan be spread around the lake but in much fewer numbers than the prolific muscovy. Even if my small army be fewer, I believed the limpkins height and girth would give us an advantage over Greybeard's horde. Without wasting another moment, I lifted off the ground and flew in the direction of Coal's territory, the leader of the limpkin clan." Mik gave a knowing look to the Sage upon hearing Coal's name but didn't interrupt his story.

"When I found Coal, there be no problem convincing him that an attack on Greybeard's territory be necessary. Coal admitted that a number of limpkin fledglings be killed by Greybeard and his minions, including several of Coal's own. Directly, Coal sent out word of a clan gathering while the thought of revenge burned through him.

When the limpkins had assembled, they all agreed that an attack on Greybeard be more than crucial. The only problem with the plan the limpkins could find be that most of the females be busy tending their clutches of chicks and wouldn't leave them to join the assault. Nevertheless, the thought of revenge ran hot in their hearts and all male limpkins agreed to join with me.

None of the limpkins be willing to squander any time for their chance of retaliation against Greybeard. Nor be I. With me in the lead our small army flew off immediately towards the direction of the Dark Marsh. It took us not long to find Greybeard in the shallow dark marshy end of the lake. The scent of the muscovy struck our nostrils long before we be in sight of Greybeard. When the large horde of enemies came into view, I be surprised to see the change in the swampy marsh. Always dark, it had turned blacker, along with the surrounding trees, and black reeds had taken up a much larger area. Even with the sun shining, a heavy cloud of darkness shrouded the entire marsh. Although the darkness blurred my eyes, I could still perceive the blue Greybeard in the center of a large flock of muscovy spread out on either side of my cousin in the form of an upside down V. I smiled to myself for the foolish tactic Greybeard had employed. Even though me and my limpkins be lesser in number we would have no trouble diving straight at Greybeard, killing him, and then destroying his malodorous crew.

I then quickly called out a loud kuuuk, the signal for the small army to follow me into a deadly assault on Greybeard. I pointed my long sharp beak directly at the heart of Greybeard as I swooped down at great speed. I felt positive that this would be the end of my hated nemesis, however, just as my beak should have struck my great enemies' heart, Greybeard moved quickly to the side, forcing me and my army to pull up and land in the pitch-like shallow water.

The muscovy now closed in around me and the limpkins. We soon found ourselves completely surrounded by stinking adversaries. Straight away I realized I had underestimated Greybeard, but before we could retreat the muscovy attacked my army and began biting at their bodies, especially their knees. Again, I had underestimated, Greybeard. It must be that he had instructed his minions on the weak points of their enemy, Greybeard himself merely stood with a smirk held on his beak watching the ferocious battle.

I fought off one muscovy after another with my long sharp beak, but I could see the brave limpkins on either side of me falling to the much larger horde of enemies. It would not be long before the only bird left to battle the muscovy wouldst be me. At that point, I suddenly heard a loud wild kuuuking cry over the cacophony of the raging battle. I could not discern where it came from until he saw a huge flock of small black moorhens with their high red forehead slamming directly into the muscovy. I also saw many of the small birds lay on their backs. They were using their wings as floats as they raised their long yellow legs ending in large claws and began tearing into the exposed breasts of the muscovy.

The fierce attack by the multitude of small black moorhens be led by Shuul and his mate Buur." The Sage stared again at Mik and announced, "they be thy great grandparents little one."

Without further comment the Sage continued. "Now the tide of the battle began to quickly switch. Everywhere around me I saw the small birds smash into the ugly muscovy and before I be aware of the change in the battle the cowardly muscovy began to lose position. Finally, in complete disarray, they paddled or flew off. The smirking beak of Greybeard now turned to hateful fright. Before I could take my revenge with one more attempt to pierce his heart, Greybeard lifted his great wings and followed by Goff, soared into darkness over the battlefield. The combat be over.

I slowly viewed my surroundings. The carnage on both sides of the battle be horrendous. On every side of me feathers of all colors floated along with the dead bodies of the combatants of both sides. Some of the injured limpkins stood on only one leg while some of the muscovy flapped one wing while the other hung loose as they attempted their escape. Most of the red beaked moorhens seemed intact. Before long, Shuul and Buur, along with another pair of leaders, made their way to me and each rubbed their black feathered necks on my badly battered legs. At that moment I knew I could never repay or forget my little black cousins.

Gradually us victors wandered from the carnage while helping those we could."

Almost out of breadth from the long tale, the Sage ended it by telling Mik that they left the cleanup to Ol' Mo.

FIVE
THE SPY

After being beaten by the young moorhen and his men driven off by the Sage, Goff knew he must return to Greybeard to face punishment for failing to carry out his order, "Kill the immature moorhen."

Goff felt tears of terror form in his eyes as he approached Greybeard lair. He had seen Greybeard use horrendous magic on his enemies, but he had no idea what terrible spell Greybeard might put upon him. It was true that his master had never committed atrocities on him, but the great blue heron had used magic to teach him to speak words for better communication.

When Goff arrived at Greybeard's haunt he was pacing back and forth with anxiety and eating grey fish from the black muck. When Goff finally stood before his master he kept his eyes low and waited to be spoken too.

"The simple task of eliminating the young moorhen has taken much time, my minion. Was the teeny bird too much for you to handle?" Greybeard asked sarcastically.

To Goff, Greybeard's voice sounded soothing but it did not chase away the chattering of his own beak. Goff stuttered with fear as he answered. "Yes, I mean no, Master. We were taken by surprise by the vicious moorhen. He attacked before I was ready. Then when we grew closer to finish him off we were surprised again by the stealthy Sage. He suddenly swooped in from above and scared many of my muscovy into flight before we could finish off the moorhen. It was not my fault. You had to be there to see the viciousness for which we were not ready. Please Master; do not use your terrible magic on me. We will try for him again when the white Sage travels south."

Greybeard's syrupy voice now turned to bitter anger. "Sage traveling to the south? You stinking fool! Where in the name of the Dark Marsh do you think Sage will be sending the little moorhen? To the south of the wide bridge, where he can keep an eye on him. You with the brains and smell of a mud turtle!"

Goff sniveled as he considered the terrible magic which was sure to be leveled against him. He attempted to plead for mercy but words would not pass through his beak. His only choice was to lower his belly and beak to the muck in a countenance which silently screamed for forgiveness.

Meanwhile, Greybeard paced before Goff with a look of deep thought and with anger in his eyes. Finally he spoke. "Listen to me, you useless dung pile. Take most of my minions and fly to the north entrance at the Wide Bridge. I want you to tightly float together like a wall in order to keep the young moorhen from beneath the bridge. After you stop him I want you to kill him. It is my guess that he comes from the family which led the charge at the marsh battle. I believed that you had already destroyed that clan, but I also feel you have failed me again. If you fail me once more it will be your harem along with you who will die.

Now, after you have assembled your minions I want you to send me five of your stoutest muscovy. As punishment for you, I want the five muscovy to bring along three of your youngest chicks. Your punishment shall be my snack."

Goff wanted to plead for his young ones but fear overwhelmed any love he felt for his many chicks. Instead, he whimpered a weak, "yes my Master," and silently slinked away to perform Greybeard's latest wicked commands.

As Greybeard watched Goff slip away he wondered if picking the large muscovy as his subordinate had been a good idea; then he decided it had not mattered. His higher self told him that one muscovy was as stupid as another. Then he calmed himself, knowing it would take some time for the dumb ducks to organize themselves enough to be able to obey his orders. To keep himself busy while he waited, Greybeard spent his time plucking one grey fish after another from the mucky marsh water and slowly slid them down his gullet.

It took much time before Greybeard noticed five large muscovy leading three small chicks across the marsh. At the sight of the chicks his mouth watered and when they reached him they quickly joined the grey fish in his stomach.

The five muscovy stood in astonishment as they watched Greybeard gobble down the three chicks. Fear of some horrible form of reprimand kept them silent as they attempted to wash the scene from their minds and waited for their orders.

Greybeard's attention now turned to the five large muscovy standing silently in fear. In a gruff voice he commanded, "You five, have you taken notice of a flock of white *Ibis* led by the one called Zignoid?"

The smell of the five muscovy was overcome by the smell of fear. None of them answered.

Greybeard waded further into the muck and closer to his minions. "I have put the spell of speech on all my minions and I find it hard to believe that all five of you have forgotten words already. I also find it hard to believe that none of you have heard of this ibis, Zignoid. I know his flock is relatively large and you must have shared space with them somewhere along the lake shore. Which of you wants to speak first or which of you wants to be turned into a wriggling grey fish first? If none of you speak, I will have five more grey fish to eat for dinner. Now one of you open your mouth and let the answer flow out."

None of the muscovy spoke until Greybeard waded closer to the largest of the five minions. "You look big enough to be an entire dinner. I hope you are not the one to speak."

Scared beyond belief, the huge muscovy opened his mouth slowly and began to talk. "I may have heard of this ibis of which you speak, Zignoid.

My cousin who lives half way to the bridge claims to have contact with a large flock of ibis led by a bird called by that name." Still in total fear, the large muscovy tried to shift the blame if he is wrong and continued. "I cannot promise that this is the flock you seek. It is not I who claims it but my cousin who makes the claim, but he might speak true."

Greybeard held a scowl on his beak but answered anyway. "I am probably as dumb as you to believe this tale; however, I will give you a chance. I want the five of you to find this Ibis called Zignoid and bring him directly to me. I have little time to spare so I want him here soon. Now go and do not return without the ibis. I feel a pang of hunger will come on soon and five fish will be needed to sooth it."

Without another word Greybeard's five minions fled across the marsh and into the sky to find Zignoid. It did not take long for the five muscovy to find the ibis and force him to fly with them to the marsh and Greybeard.

Greybeard was happy to meet Zignoid and seemed to offer a friendly greeting. No sooner had Zignoid appeared before Greybeard when the great blue heron ordered the four smallest muscovy to grasp hold of the ibis' two wings and legs. He then ordered the largest fifth muscovy to come before him.

The largest minion was still queasy about being in the presence of Greybeard but he obeyed the order. Greybeard looked down on the largest of the muscovy and spoke. "What are you called, large one? I have a task for you and if you complete it well, in the future you might be rewarded." Less frightened, the muscovy spoke up. "I am called Jull and I have the second largest harem in the clan next to Goff. What task do you ask of me?"

"A simple one really, Jull." Greybeard answered in a soothing tone. "I wish you to pluck a small grey feather from my beard and stuff it up the nostril of Zignoid. Can you do that simple task for me, Jull?"

The fear intensified in Jull at the thought of touching the malicious great blue heron. Although the thought of a future reward pushed him passed his terror and he reached up with his beak and pulled out the smallest grey feather he could find in his Master's beard. He then went to the struggling ibis and stuffed the feather up his nostril and stood back.

The effect the feather had on Zignoid was striking. His beak turned grey and soon, so did his feathers; then he fell unconscious. It was not long before his beak and feathers turned to their original color and Zignoid stood on his feet. He looked the same except his eyes had turned from blue to a deep grey. The heron waded close to him, looked down and spoke. "Can you hear and understand me, Zignoid of the ibis?" The much smaller bird looked up and nodded in affirmation.

"That is good," said Greybeard and continued. "Are you willing to accept me as your Master and to follow my orders?" Again another nod from Zignoid. "That is good Zignoid. Are you ready to accept my commands now?" Still another nod from the ibis up to Greybeard who again answered good and continued. "Listen carefully ibis. What I want of you is to fly back to your flock, lead them across the Wide Bridge and land on a grassy knoll to the left of the lake. Can you do that?" Another nod and another command from Greybeard. "All you must do is feed on the knoll and fly to me with reports of any unusual activity you see. Can you do that?" Another nod and Zignoid flew off in a great nervous rush back to his flock.

SIX
UNDER THE BRIDGE

Throughout his growth to near adulthood, Mik experienced many of the problems the Sage had predicted. He was always troubled by flashbacks of his family's destruction and had many adventures in his attempt to survive. These included close calls with alligators, snakes, and more Ol' Mo type turtles than he cared to remember, as well as fights with almost any bird in order to seek attention. Yet he always felt steeped in deep depression from the low self-esteem he tried to hide with his outward brashness. It took Mik almost too full maturity to even begin to consider the thought of traveling through the darkness under the Wide Bridge.

On the north side of the bridge he had grown used to many horrifying rumors of the southern side of the bridge, which had found his ears. In his imagination, each rumor grew larger, to the point that the passage through the darkness under the bridge was like the passage into the land of death. Mik feared that the other side must be inhabited by creatures even worse than Ol' Mo or more gators or even more like Greybeard and his minions. He also heard that the other side was inhabited by large hawks that for a quick lunch could easily carry him off, as well as of water moccasins longer than the Sage who could poison him and at their leisure, eat him. In his mind he felt there was no need to struggle with more new dangers. Even though other moorhens never let him enter their territory or come near their females, he could still find enough food so he didn't starve. Besides, he had lots of fun chasing female brown mottled ducks who would fly off in terror when he lowered his head and he swam in their direction. No, he felt grown enough to know what was good for him no matter what the Sage had suggested.

However, now the great Sage had left Mik with little choice. He had been told of the brave exploits of his grandparents, Shuul and Buur. This fact helped him gather the courage to defeat his fears and consider a plunge through the dark waters under the foreboding bridge. With his new found inner strength, Mik finally pushed his long yellow legs south towards the darkness he feared he would find under the Wide Bridge.

As Mik bobbed closer to the passage, his nerve began to falter. The dark opening under the bridge was blocked by a long line of wing to wing minions of Greybeard. In the center of the line floated the largest of the muscovy, Goff. Without thinking, Mik's paddling legs automatically halted. Quickly his eyes sought a rout around the ugly horde, but none could be found. Finally, the memory of the words the Sage had told him about the courage of his grandparents gave him the final resolve to find another solution. It came to him in a flash along with the frantic paddling of his long yellow legs. With his head down, Mik pushed himself as fast as possible directly at the center of the pack, and Goff. Mik appeared ready to smash into the huge muscovy for the second time, but at the last instant he made a sharp left turn and crashed through the wings of the next two minions and sailed quickly into the black maw beneath the bridge.

As the darkness took over from the light under the bridge, Mik paused to listen for followers. He heard none; the muscovy had less courage than him. The pure blackness surrounding him threw terror through his mind as if seeing the death of his family once again. He wanted to turn back and live in the world he knew. But what about the Sage? Could he ever face the Sage again if he lost his courage and fled? He finally decided that he feared the disgrace when facing the Sage more than what lay ahead. With a huge gulp of air, he pushed his fears aside and bobbed into the darkness ahead.

At first he could only smell damp mustiness which pervaded the entire inside of the wide old moldy structure. The further he bobbed, the darker it became, until only darkness surrounded him. Mik was blind. Fortunately his keen senses helped him to feel what lay beneath the dark water. Mostly, he sensed large swarms of what he had learned were black whiskered catfish. About them he had no worry. They were bottom feeders and would barely notice him as he bobbed overhead. What he really feared were the large bats he knew were somewhere in the darkness above, and largemouth bass.

He knew it was the bat's other-worldliness that scared him, but he really didn't believe a bat was about to attack a bird. But the bass were something else. With their size, speed, and razor sharp teeth they could sweep in from anywhere and cut a grown moorhen's neck in half. He could be aware of any big fish around but the bigmouth's speed could easily avoid his senses. Constantly fighting off fear, his heart leapt with elation when he could make out the faint light at the other end of the cavernous stone passageway.

Mik was only the distance of the length of two great white herons from bright sunshine on the south side of the bridge when the ominous swish of an enormous largemouth bass splashed from the dark waters. If Mik's head hadn't been bobbing backwards the bass would have taken it off. Without an instant's thought his web-less legs found the last of his strength and churned swiftly, finally driving him into the bright sunshine where he breathed a deep sigh of relief. He had escaped the old world and also once again, death.

Mik's first glance told him he really had entered a new world. The lake on the other side of the bridge was much wider with plenty of reeds for food and shelter. His senses could not feel any immediate danger, but he did spy several moorhens along the shore, especially those who appeared to be single females. He also took note of some of the other inhabitants. On a rock not far away he spotted a large turtle sunning himself. A further distance away was a *great white egret*. He was not about to tangle with that bird unless it was in defense of a future family. Amongst some of the other moorhens he noticed a tall, long legged wading bird he knew as a limpkin. Just as when he was with the Sage, Mik felt he had no reason for fear of the large bird and guessed the limpkin was only searching for food or a mate. It was that season. A ways out from the shore he noticed a few mottled ducks but he didn't think of them as more than sport. Far across the lake he saw a tall stand of bamboo. He felt a strange affinity towards it but didn't give it much thought, besides, his stomach was telling him it was time for food and he headed for a clump of reeds further on and hoped for a satisfying lunch.

As he entered the thick reeds he found himself staring at the raised rear end of an older moorhen. He knew from past experience he had invaded the territory of another of his kind. To make it even worse, he noticed a female hidden behind the threatening older moorhen and decided his best choice was to make a hasty retreat. He already knew how fierce a moorhen could be while defending their territory and mate.

Mik quickly bobbed along the reeds until he located an opening leading to the shore. He felt he was no coward but he did look around carefully for other mating moorhens or possibly any other hidden predator. Seeing nothing dangerous, he hopped up on the shore and began pecking at some newly sprouted grass and a few insects. He felt relaxed and let his keen senses be swept away as he thought about what the great battle between the Sage and Greybeard must have been like. As usual he was bothered by the image of his family being destroyed by the alligator.

Suddenly, danger pulled Mik from his thoughts and he looked up from his pecking to see what he had heard about but had never seen one, a humongous *iguana*. It had a red neck that hung to the ground and was staring him in the eyes. Mik was about to go into a defensive stance when the huge creature bobbed the thick skin around his throat and lumbered on his four stubby legs around Mik, as if Mik didn't exist.

As the huge iguana moved off into the bushes seeking a mate, Mik scurried quickly to the water and the safety of the thick reeds. He stayed motionless in the reeds for a while, wondering why the large iguana didn't eat him. Then he remembered the Sage had told him not to fear the big ugly lizards. The Sage had said, "The only thing they ate be flowers." With his senses reawakened, Mik began to move and discover more about his new home.

When Mik reached open water again he saw that the turtle was still sleeping in the sun and decided to have a little fun. He bobbed over to the sleeping turtle and snuck quietly behind him. Then with a quick swish of his wing, he splashed the sleeping turtle with water. The turtle, who was startled awake, gave Mik a killing look as the moorhen bobbed off with a few strokes of his long legs and a smiling gesture on his beak.

What Mik didn't see was a gaggle of female moorhens on a small rise at the edge of the lake some distance away. Being mating season, the females couldn't help notice the single moorhen male that had come from under the bridge. It was a rare occurrence because it was common knowledge that horrible creatures lived on the bridge's northern side.

The thing Mik did notice was a bush hanging over the lake. The bush was full of red berries, some almost touching the water. What was strange was the fact that the berries were half dried but not yet eaten. He thought that the berries would be a treat for any bird and bobbed over to see what they might taste like.

All the while, his behavior was being observed by the female moorhens, especially one called, Bek, who was the leader of the gaggle. She acted as if she believed she were a queen and if any of the other females didn't obey her every wish she sometimes made them eat dirt. They all knew of how strong and independent she could be, and they all had heard the story about when she was a mere fledgling. Her older brother from an earlier clutch in her family had been surrounded by three bullying muscovy ducks. Without a thought of her own safety, Bek had rushed from the protective reeds and with rapid flapping of her short wings and a wild kuuuking screech chased the stinking bullies away. Among the other moorhens, Bek's reputation for courage grew tremendously, along with any other bird on the lake who heard the story.

Mik wasn't thinking anything about dirt or any other story as he got closer to the bush full of berries. He heard his stomach growl louder the closer he got to the sight of the sun ripened fruit. When he finally reached them, he ripped off the closest berry to the water. It had an odd sweet taste to it which warmed his throat after it passed his beak. He knew he had never had any berries like these on the old side of the bridge and believed this must have been what the Sage meant when he spoke of the wonders of the new world. Without wasting any more time Mik gobbled down every berry he could reach.

Suddenly a strange feeling hit his stomach and made its way to his head. He had never felt this way before and realized his surroundings started to look strange. In some cases single objects became double. He now saw two turtles sunning on the rock. In his drunken state Mik decided the two turtles must be conspiring against him. Without a second thought he dashed across the lake ready to smash his adversaries, but before he reached them the lone turtle slid off the rock and into the water. Mik crashed straight into the rock. Now he was really dazed, but not so much that he didn't see the moorhen and his mate appear from the reeds. He remembered humiliating himself earlier by not taking up the challenge of the other bird and bobbed directly at him for a second try. Again, the other bird turned and raised his tail feathers in warning. Without a pause Mik ran across the water directly at the raised tail feathers of the other moorhen but never noticed the fact that his opponents' sharp claws were also exposed. Having missed the sight of the claws, Mik barreled straight into them, thus receiving two minor warning scratches on his chest. It was not a serious wound, but enough to bring some of his senses back and he quickly retreated.

Mik now bobbed in circles trying to understand what was wrong. On his fourth circle he spotted a small iguana on the shore. Still in a senseless state, he charged full speed at the lizard on the shore. Before he reached the iguana his long feet tripped on the shallow ground on shore and he fell straight on his beak. Fortunate for Mik in his inebriated state he couldn't hear the squawks of laughter coming from the gaggle of females still watching him from the rise near the shoreline.

His beak aching, Mik felt more berries were what he needed to ease his pain so he bobbed directly to the bush with the berries. Unfortunately for him, all the berries were too high to reach, so he backed further out on the lake in order to make a jump for the higher berries. He was able to make the jump but his thin body ended up flying past the berries and deeply into the bush where he found himself pinned on all sides. More squawks of laughter came from the shore but he couldn't turn his head to see from where they came.

It took Mik what he believed to be a long time to work his way out of the bush; however, one compensation was that he got to eat more berries before he eventually dropped back into the lake. Now he felt the buzz in his head again, along with a feeling for mating. At first, all he could see was a cluster of mottle ducks out on the open water and wasted no time before he bobbed straight at them with the idea that he didn't care what kind of mate he needed; however, he found himself going in all directions as each duck he came near took flight in fear. Before long he could see that they were all gone.

SEVEN

MIK MEETS BEK

After the mottle ducks had all flown off Mik heard the squawking of laughter again. This time he was able to turn his head and see the gaggle of female moorhens on the rise of the bank. He should have been furious but his senses were numb and again he headed straight for the squawking. When he reached the shoreline, he charged robustly up the shore at the females. Most scrambled for the water and Mik chased all of them. He attempted to nibble on all of their necks but they were easily able to paddle quickly out of his reach. Finally he had had it. The rush from the berries has subsided along with his energy. He could merely float in the water watching the young female moorhens scattering in all directions.

Unexpectedly, he noticed one of the noisy moorhens was still standing on the raised bank of the shore. He felt sure she must be the one who would become his and as usual the impetuous Mischief paddled straight for her. As his feet touched the shore he began the climb up the steep bank. He soon realized his legs were a little wobbly due to the berries, but he thought nothing could stop him now.

When he finally reached the top of the bank he wasted no time at beginning the mating ritual. He opened his beak to nip the neck of the one he believed would soon be his mate. Suddenly, he found his eyes and mouth filled with dirt kicked at him by a long yellow leg of the staunchly standing female moorhen. Shaken by the choking and blindness caused by the dirt, he stepped back in confusion. When Mik finally coughed the last of the black obstruction from his throat and the tears cleared from his eyes, he looked straight into the infuriated face of the most beautiful female moorhen his swollen eyes have ever seen. In an instant that image disappeared as a swift movement of her short wing hit the wobbly Mik and knocked him directly back down the bank and into the water.

From her perch on the bank, Bek looked angrily down at the dirty and now soaked Mik and kuuuked her contempt. "How dare you approach me you wild ruffian, you crazy scoundrel, you horny rascal from the other side of the bridge. Don't you know that female moorhens pick the mate and we prefer those with thick bodies who can help incubate our broods? We don't want a runt who couldn't even warm a lizard egg. We've been watching you and your drunken ways and there's no female on this side of the bridge who wants to have anything to do with you. We know your kind. All you want is one thing. And besides, you look like swamp trash and smell worse than a muscovy."

From the drenching in the water, Mik's head finally cleared of the last of the buzz created by the fermented berries. Although he found her the most beautiful moorhen he has ever seen, he didn't care about what she believed. His anger had raised to its crest and he kuuuked back at her. "Well you look worse than iguana dung and smell like a bog full of mud turtles."

As usual Mik's anger overwhelmed him as he righted himself. On much stronger legs he scrambled back up the bank to give that brazen female the thrashing she deserved. He soon climbed over the rise only to find her waiting with white tail feathers raised and ready for a fight to the death.

Unexpectedly they both heard the sound of whooshing feathers and both stood in bewilderment as the huge regal white Sage landed between them. As if it were thunder, the rumbling of the Sage's voice spoke to them both. "What be going on here? Doth thou two birds not know who thou be and who you came from? The behavior of the both of thee shames the memory of the leaders of both thou clans going back to the *Battle of the Dark Marsh*. Do you not understand that it be both thy duty to join together and raise a force of the strongest moorhens on either side of the bridge in order to defeat Greybeard and his minions.

With each moon the power of the Dark Marsh grows stronger. At this moment all life coming in contact with the dark evil of the marsh has withered and died or be fleeing to safer territory. Thou hath no idea how soon that horrible black cloud wouldst hang over thy heads.

As thee stand to brawl, more of the northern end of the lake hath already diminished. Even the mightiest of alligators cannot stand against the vile magic of the great blue heron, Greybeard, and the foul dark marsh he draws with him. If thou seeks not to unite I fear for the eventual safety of all living creatures on and around our beautiful peaceful home."

The size and grandeur of the Sage caused both Mik and Bek to cringe in their shame. Neither could find words to answer the great white heron. They could merely bend their necks in a fife-like bow to their powerful cousin. As their necks were bent, an eye of each moorhen poked around the yellow legs of the Sage in order to make another appraisal of the bird they were just about to pummel. Neither of them had lost their anger, nor did they kuuuk.

Finally the deafening silence ended when the booming voice of the Sage thundered once again. "Mik and Bek, thou be the two. The ones to save the lake, Mik, the grandson of Shuul and Buur and you Bek, granddaughter of Puul and Juul, those leaders who didst sooth my wounds after the great Battle of the Dark Marsh. It is thou who whilst mate in order to make us all free and safe once again.

Fear not little ones; I pledge my honor and life as thy guide through the troubling times I see ahead. I shall help Mik to shed the problems caused by watching the demise of his family. And you dear Bek, I shall be the one to help thee lose thy shrew-like temperament which causes fear in all those who wouldst wish the great love you hold deep within thyself. I shall guide thee to a safe location. Teach thee both to survive the trials of the lake. But most of all I shall teach thee how to defeat Greybeard and keep the Dark Marsh from spreading its ugly evil over us all."

The Sage's wings pushed both birds together expecting them to stroke each other neck to neck. Instead, what he saw was Bek reach out with her short wing and strike Mik across the face. In return Mik struck Bek in the leg as hard as possible with his yellow clawed foot. The screaming between the two began again.

Finally, in total exasperation, the Sage spread his massive wings to split apart the battling moorhens and spoke harshly. "I doth see that thou both need more time to reconcile. The mating of thou be of much more importance than thy petty squabbles. I be seeing a plan that I believe will cool thee both down. Unfortunately it will take some time for the plan to take effect. Now, listen to me. I be taking Mik to the other side of the lake to begin a program which will help his temperament. And thee, Bek, will stay in this place where I shall return in a short while to begin a program for thee."

Bek spoke to the Sage in sharp words. "You are wasting your time wise bird. The deepest program of which you propose would have to be deeper than this lake for me to have anything to do with this scrawny scamp. I should rather spend my days with a stinking muscovy than spend a minute with this brawling maniac from under the bridge!"

Mik was about to unfold another verbal attack aimed at the angry female, but before he could voice his caustic words, they were stifled in his throat by the large white wing of the Sage covering his face. Angrily, the Sage spoke directly to Mik. "Listen to me carefully little moorhen, I be flying across the lake, now! You will watch for me in the sky and bob behind." Mik began to protest but a sharp look prevented any contradiction.

The Sage than turned to Bek. "As for thee, miss shrew, I expect thou to be right here when I be returning and I need not hear another kuuuk from thy sharp beak about it. Dost I be understood?" Bek said nothing. She merely turned her back and lowered her head. The Sage knew her movement was consent to his angry kuuuk and she did not dare kuuuk another sound. Immediately, the great wings of the Sage spread and he lifted into the air.

Without another glance at Bek, Mik quickly climbed down the bank. He looked up in the direction the Sage flew and followed as fast as his long yellow legs would move.

As Bek stood on the rise next to the lake and Mik followed the Sage, none of them had taken any notice of a typical flock of Ibis which had landed on the nearby grassy knoll during their melee. Neither did they notice that as the Sage took flight, so did the leader of the flock, Zignoid. Zignoid did not follow the Sage, instead he flew north over the Wide Bridge in the direction of the lair of Greybeard.

EIGHT

ZIGNOID'S REPORT

Before Zignoid took off in flight to Greybeard's lair he had instructed his flock to stay put until he returned. They were to continue to munch on what grubs or worms they might find on the grassy knoll, but they were also to keep an eye on the lake for any unusual behavior.

After Zignoid had flown across the Wide Bridge, he noticed a large flock of muscovy ducks squabbling amongst themselves, but mostly their anger seemed to be aimed at the largest bird in the group. He assumed that they must be the muscovy Greybeard had sent out to stop a young moorhen from passing under the bridge. From his observations from the grassy knoll he figured one of the battling moorhens he had observed talking with the great white must have been that particular bird. He had no idea what action Greybeard might take due to the muscovy failure but before he found out, he hoped to make his report and return to the flock. At any rate, before he had passed them the squawking had died down after a couple of swats on some heads by the wing of the largest in the group. Then, as he was about to pass out of sight, he saw them moving hurriedly in the same direction in which he was flying.

The flight seemed long but finally Zignoid recognized the darkness of the marsh before him. Behind the marsh he could make out a small patch of blue that even at a distance he knew must be Greybeard and flew directly to him.

When Zignoid landed near the huge bird he was nervous. Greybeard was walking back and forth in his nesting area deep in thought and Zignoid felt afraid to interrupt him. He didn't have to; after a short wait and without looking at him, Greybeard gruffly asked what he had found out. Zignoid knew his master would not like his answer and found his beak was unable to give a reply due to its violent quivering.

Greybeard had little patience for the long beaked white bird and said so. "Stop your quivering you piece of snail snot. Speak at once or I'll feed you to hungry god of the Dark Marsh. I know he would love some white meat. Now stop your quivering and speak up!"

Zignoid's fear overcame his quivering beak and sounds finally stammered from his long curved beak. "I...I...I have news that may not please you Master. You seem not to be in a mood to receive it so maybe I should tell you later."

Greybeard quickly replied, "There will be no later time for you, stupid worm eater. Tell me of what you have seen before I turn you into a crayfish!"

Wishing to bury himself into the mud to avoid Greybeard's anger, Zignoid almost whispered his answer. "Well, Master Greybeard, I think I might have seen the young moorhen you were seeking on the south side of the straight bridge." Zignoid could not look directly at the blue heron.

"You must have seen more, you cowardly creature," Greybeard growled. "Was he with anyone? Did you hear words from his beak? I order you. Tell me more!"

The ibis screwed up his courage and explained that he saw the male moorhen have a fight with a strong willed female moorhen but it was broken up by a great white heron. Then he said that the heron flew off, followed by the male moorhen, and the female was left standing alone by the side of the lake. "I know not what they said from the distance I stood but it appeared that the great white somehow knew the other two birds. I did hear something about the takeover of the lake. I'm sorry my Master but that is all I can report." But then to shift some of the blame, Zignoid babbled that while he was flying to make his report he noticed a flock of arguing muscovy led by one very large duck. "I truly believe they are coming this way." Zignoid's final words could hardly be heard.

Terrified, Zignoid shook with dread as he watched the huge great blue heron break into an insane rage. He believed for sure he had lived his last breath and would have tried to flee if his feet hadn't felt glued in the mud. Suddenly, he saw the flock of muscovy in the distance led by the largest of the group. Greybeard saw them also and suddenly his rage quieted like the lake after a storm. Greybeard and Zignoid both waited in silence until the muscovy had almost approached. Unexpectedly, Greybeard turned to

Zignoid and ordered him to find the muscovy named, Jull. He instructed Zignoid to tell Jull to round up the entire harem of Goff, including all their chicks, and for Jull to bring them all to the Dark Marsh at once. "And Zignoid, after you give my instructions to Jull, I want you to return directly to the marsh. I have a special treat I want you to observe."

Zignoid gave a quick nod to Greybeard and flew off toward a large flock of muscovy he had observed on the shoreline on his way south to the marsh. It soothed his nerves to leave the Greybeard. He only regretted that he must return. As Zignoid flew off on his new mission, he saw that the muscovy, led by Goff, were drawing nearer to Greybeard who had waded out to the center of the marsh.

Goff halted any forward movement at the edge of the dark water, along with the other muscovy at his back. He noticed the white ibis flying off and guessed that the long beaked bird had already explained that he had spied the young moorhen on the south side of the straight bridge. Immediately, he decided to drop his excuse that the little moorhen had used magic to break a hole in his brigade and flee into the darkness under the bridge. Instead, Goff felt a fearful shiver begin to spread through his body.

Finally, Greybeard spoke to Goff in a quiet patient voice. "I have already heard word of you having failed me again, dear Goff. Why don't you leave your troop behind and paddle over to me so I may hear the dreadful story from the muscovy's own beak."

At first Goff was to afraid to move, but eventually lack of malice in his Master's voice led him to paddle skittishly towards the sound of Greybeard. When he reached within a two wing distance from the great blue he abruptly stopped, slowly looked up at Greybeard and waited for his masters' next command. As he waited, Goff noticed the ibis land in the mud at the bank of the marsh.

Greybeard said nothing for awhile, although Goff could now see nothing but craven maliciousness in his eyes. Finally he spoke. "Now my dear Goff, I have arranged a special surprise for you, especially since you have returned with grief in your heart and sorrow in your eyes for not capturing or killing one young bird who you outsize by almost five times." The tone in Greybeard's voice began to grow slowly to a violent rage. Just as Goff thought for sure he was about to lose his head, the rage in Greybeard's voice suddenly dropped to a drawling friendliness once again. "Now Goff, I want you to turn around and see what a wonderful greeting home I prepared just for you."

With one paddle of his large webbed foot Goff turned to see, waiting on the edge of the marsh, his entire harem along with all their chicks. He also noticed they were corralled into two separate groups by Jull. The troop who had accompanied him to the Straight Bridge had pulled back further from the marsh and merely floated in a frightened knot.

Greybeard spoke in a pleasing voice once again. "Jull, would you please send Goff's love chicks over here so they might greet their father with a lovingly warm homecoming." Jull quickly marshaled Goff's many chicks into a single file and sent them into the marsh in the direction of their father.

Goff watched as the long line of pliant young ones filed obediently towards him. Just as the first chick was a mere wing away from him, Goff felt a strong tug on his feet. The closer his chicks approached, the stronger the tug became on his feet, until he realized he was slowly being pulled down into the repulsive black muck that was the Dark Marsh. With every movement he made to free himself the further down he sank. Even a worse horror now occurred before his fright-filled eyes. As his young chicks approached him, Goff noticed that Greybeard was standing beside him. With every chick that approached, Greybeard's extensive neck shot out his beak and he swallowed each of the chicks down his lengthy gullet. By the time Goff had seen his last little one vanish down that blue feathered throat, all but his eyes and beak rose above the black muck. His last action before he plunged below the marshy blackness was a screech of horror from his disappearing beak.

The flock at the edge of the marsh floated in shocked stillness. All were horrified by the gruesome scene they had just observed. Even those who had witnessed the terrible cruelness of Greybeard's behavior could not believe their eyes. Nevertheless, no one could find the courage or fearlessness to move or make a sound.

What they all did hear now was the roaring sound of the magical great blue heron. "Hear me all of you who have gathered at this scene. This was but a small taste of what anyone who fails to carry out any order given by me will endure. Listen all! I am the master of this lake and if I proclaim that you must die for me, you must die. I have great plans for this whole lake, including south of the Wide Bridge, and I expect complete obedience from every one of you, even to the death.

Now you, the harem of Goff, I expect your sniveling to end here. I also expect you to join the harem of Jull; that means today. We need a huge army for my plans and you shall provide it. And you, the cowards who let a tiny moorhen slip through your wings, I expect you all to join with Jull, the commander of my new army. Those who do not will find themselves swallowed by the *Dark Marsh* as was Goff. Am I not understood?" Not a sound was heard. Only the stink of fear pervaded the air.

Next, Greybeard turned to Zignoid. "You, long-beaked piece of snot. Fly with all your strength quickly back to your flock and once again I order you to report any change south of the bridge directly to me; now fly."

Zignoid wasted no time getting off the ground and towards his flock. When he turned back to see the results of what he had so recently experienced, he saw the Master return to his lair; a large black bubble rise and burst over the marsh, the minions of Goff joining with Jull, and the harem of Goff fighting to be the first to have chicks with their new leader and commander, Jull.

NINE

BEK

Bek turned and watched the Sage and the scruffy moorhen until they were mere dots on the other side of the lake. She then turned back and looked along the shoreline until she spotted a thick expanse of reeds in front of a large overgrown bush. She knew that deep beneath that bush lay a large nest. It was in that nest where she began her life and she did not remember it with fondness.

A pair of mating moorhens can produce three clutches of eggs per season and each clutch was generally three to six eggs. Both parents take turns incubating the brood. When the chicks crack out of their shells they are called hatchlings. When they are old enough to leave the nest they are called fledglings, until they become mature enough to care for themselves.

Bek hatched first in the second clutch of four eggs that season. Her mother, Kreeb, and her father, Raab, both shared incubating the clutch and were devoted to all their hatchlings. When Bek was still a hatchling, Kreeb and Raab produced still a third clutch of six more eggs; there was little room in the nest. To make matters worse, Bek's mother, Kreeb, had a close sister, Gree. Kreeb and Gree had hatched simultaneously, the only hatchlings to break free of their shells out of five eggs. As would be expected, the sisters grew extremely close. When Gree told Kreeb that her mate had been lost in a storm and she needed a safe place to have her first brood of eggs, Kreeb felt she had no choice but to make room in her already crowded nest for the three eggs Gree soon produced.

Raab and Kreeb continued to feed and care for their hatchlings while Gree stayed in the nest incubating her eggs. Most of the time Raab went searching for food himself while the two females guarded the crowded nest.

One morning Raab left the nest early in order to get a head start on gathering food for his growing family. It wasn't long before Kreeb began to notice her mate had not yet returned. The hatchlings were all peeping loudly for food as Gree sat comfortably on her thee eggs. Gree constantly complained that the peeping could bring predators.

By the time the sun had reached directly overhead and the sound of the hatchlings was at a shrieking pitch, Kreeb knew something serious must be wrong. Raab had never been missing that long since they had mated. She had to leave the hatchlings with her sister and search for her mate. She explained the situation to Gree, climbed from the nest and pushed her way through the reeds and out onto the lake.

Once on the open lake Kreeb glanced quickly around and found nothing out of line. A few mottled ducks dove for food not far away, a small family of limpkins were pecking on the lakeshore and a number of single male and female moorhens were checking each other out as possible mates. Her only choice was to approach the moorhens and find out if they had seen anything of her mate, Raab. No answer was positive and her only real option was to quickly gather some food for her starving hatchlings and head back to the nest.

When Kreeb reached the nest and allowed the fresh food to quiet the young ones, she heard more startling sound from Gree. Gree told her she had felt movement in the shells beneath her and that she believed her brood was about to hatch. Kreeb was again out of options. She wanted to search for her mate and yet she knew if Gree's hatchlings broke out, they both must eat their shells quickly lest a predator smell the birth shell and find the nest full of defenseless hatchlings. Almost immediately the three hatchlings broke free of their eggs and both female moorhens gobbled the shells as fast as they could get them down.

By the time they finished their unpleasant task, the sun was still barely in the sky. That left only enough time for Kreeb to go searching for food as the hatchling peeps were beginning to rise once again and there would be no time to look for Raab. That task would have to wait until morning; and even worse, the grief of possibly having lost her mate was already beginning to crawl into her heart.

Kreeb split the night watch over the nest with Gree, but early the next morning she left the nest to gather food as quickly as possible. After she and Gree had fed the hatchlings, Kreeb went directly back out on the lake in search of Raab. This time she decided to search all the reeds to see if he was possibly hurt and thus unable to make it back to the nest.

Kreeb was only partly around the lake and deep into an unfamiliar growth of reeds. At the time all her attention was on finding Raab. She did not see or sense that another animal was also in the reeds, O'l Mo. *His* only interest was finding his next meal. That meal bobbed straight into his jaws without even a thought of resistance.

Back at the nest the gaggle of hatchlings were beginning their ritual of peeping for food. Gree knew the sound would only grow louder and so far there was no accounting of where her sister might be. As the peeping grew louder, Gree's natural motherly instinct told her she must leave the nest alone to find food for the now screeching hatchlings. The oldest of the hatchlings was Bek. Gree knew the young moorhen would be of no help if a raccoon or alligator found the nest, but she had no other choice. As best as she could, she explained to Bek what was expected of her and quickly left to find food or possibly her sister.

As Bek watched Gree climbing out of the nest she realized that she was now responsible for twelve screaming hatchlings, plus herself. She knew nothing of mothering or of taking care of little ones. All she knew was that they all must be screeching because they were as hungry as she was. Quickly looking around, she saw tiny pieces of shells that had been missed by her mother and aunt. Because she had seen Kreeb and Gree eat the shells she assumed they that must be some kind of food. Without thinking, she picked up a scrap of shell and dropped it in the mouth of the closest little one. It seemed to quiet its screeching for a time, so she searched for more shell, and as she found a piece she again dropped it into another little beak. She found more shells and kept dropping them into the closest open beak until all were quiet. The silence didn't last long. Soon she heard a single peep, and then another and another until an entire cacophony of peeping began to drive her mad. Unexpectedly, Bek realized something wet was falling from her eyes and she inherently knew she was becoming overwhelmed by the anxiety of too much responsibility for her tender age.

Ultimately, Bek noticed a tiny mite crawling across the bottom of the nest. She snatched it up and threw it into the closest beak. She began to look for more mites and found them. More insects flew into the hatchling beaks. She was about to eat the last one herself when her aunt Gree jumped back into the nest with a mouthful of seeds which she began to stuff into the open beaks of her own thee hatchlings. What was left over she dumped into the beaks of the other little ones, but when it came to Bek there was nothing left accept one tiny mite crawling at the bottom of the nest. It would have to make due.

The routine kept up for days, with Bek taking care of a clutch of chicks and Gree taking care of her own three chicks first; whatever food was left she tossed onto the bottom of the nest for Bek to feed her brothers and sisters. Occasionally there was some food left for Bek, and if not, she managed to find enough mites to keep herself alive.

One day Gree was late coming back with food. Bek was left alone with twelve screeching hatchlings and no mites. She was about to begin screeching like the rest of the clutch when an idea fell into her young mind. She had started to watch how aunt Gree crawled over the edge of the nest when leaving. Bek had no idea about what was on the other side of what she perceived as a great wall, but she knew she could take no more of the unbearably crowded, noisy nest and the overwhelming responsibilities that went with it. Without thinking further, Bek used her tiny beak and small clawed toes to slowly push and pull herself over the great wall, and then found herself falling off the top into a bed of leaves.

Bek worked her way to her feet and took the first look around. Her mind was boggled. The immenseness of everything surrounding her almost scared her into attempting a climb back into the nest. The only thing that stopped her from attempting to go back over the top was a stand of reeds next to the nest and on those reeds were seeds, food.

She pecked as fast as she could at the unripe seeds until she could peck no more. For the first time since she lost her mother and father her stomach felt full. But it didn't last long as her belly began to wretch and the unripe seeds poured from her beak. When she thought she had gone through the worst things in her short life, she heard Gree coming through the reeds. She knew Gree had a short temper and if she was caught it most likely would be the end of her life. Quickly she dove under another pile of leaves and listened until she heard Gree grunt as she climbed the wall. What she than heard was the hungry wail of the starving hatchlings, but no call for Bek. She guessed Gree would never miss another beak she would have to feed.

Feeling it was safe to come out of hiding, Bek left and scrambled for the cover of a low hanging bush. She stayed put until her starving stomach told her she could wait no longer to eat. Suddenly, at her feet she saw what looked like a large mite crawl out of the ground. She didn't know what it was but her hunger made her eat it. Soon appeared another and her stomach was able to hold down the insects. She stayed in that one spot until fear told her it was time to move on before she became food for something else.

As moons passed, Bek's senses taught her what she could and could not eat. She also wandered further and further from the nest until one day she poked her head threw a screen of reeds and was astounded at the open space of waves moving in a rhythm which seemed like the color of the sky but had no sun. She looked further out and saw creatures like herself but large like Kreeb and Raab. The real astonishment was the fact that sailing through the sky were birds much larger than her parents and of almost any color imaginable. One of the larger creatures looked her way and she bolted up on the shore of what she later would learn was the *lake*. She had a natural passion to see herself out on the lake, but nature told her she was still much too young for that.

Bek learned to spend much of her time hiding and eating in the deep reeds, but she also spent some time looking through the reeds and noticed more birds that looked like her mother and father. She watched them carefully and noticed that when they were at the edge of the lake they would duck their heads under the blue and come out with snails and sprouts, just like those that Gree occasionally gave to her and the chicks, which they would quickly eat. This led Bek to get her feet wet, along with finding a new source of food. She even found herself wading further into the water until she realized she could lift her feet and float like the others, but something told her it was unsafe to come out of the reeds as of yet.

One day after feeding she stepped onto the shore towards the pile of leaves she had begun to think of as home. No sooner had she headed in the right direction when a loud hissing sound stopped her in her tracks. Coming directly at her slithered a long slimy creature with no legs but with a white mouth wide open. The opening was aimed directly at her and she instinctively knew she was done for. The slithering monster was to close for her to rush for cover and her fear held her in place with the hope she would blend into the forest. She didn't. The jaws of the monster hung above her and it would soon be over; but it wasn't. Suddenly she saw a pair of huge claws attached to yellow legs wrap themselves around the monster and it was pulled away into the sky. She didn't know what had just happened but she rushed to her home of leaves and let water roll from her eyes until time allowed the fear to subside and she fell into a deep sleep.

One day not long after her near life ending encounter, she heard a familiar high pitched kuuuk coming from the other side of the reeds. The sound was young but she thought she remembered it from the nest and the clutch of hatchlings that came before her brood. It sounded like it might be an older brother. All those hatchlings had grown to fledglings and had left the nest while she was still a hatchling, but she still remembered the familiar tone from the nest. Another thing she noticed was a horrible smell. The smell was so bad it almost kept her curiosity from looking through the reeds for the familiar sound. She heard the squeaky kuuuk once more and couldn't control her curiosity any longer. She poked her small head out of the reeds to the open lake and saw a bird somewhat bigger than her but of the same kind. The problem was, the young bird was surrounded by three huge ducks she hadn't seen before. The ducks were menacing the smaller bird and it appeared they were about to kill the little one. Bek didn't know what struck her. Maybe it was the loneliness she felt or possibly the small one was a brother or even possibly the fact that a tremendous rage had built up in her due to having too much responsibility at a young age.

She really didn't think much about it. The only thing she felt was the terrible rage and the need to help the one who could be a brother. Before she knew it she came screeching out of the reeds, her beak down low and her growing legs paddling madly at the group of stinking birds. The large birds were startled to the point that they knew not what was happening or how many more of those crazy black birds might be coming their way. None of them wasted any time taking flight and the lake soon contained only two small black birds, brother and sister.

TEN
MINDFULNESS COMES TO THE LAKE

As Bek tucked away the bad memories of her early life, she looked up to see the Sage flying her way. Soon he swept down beside her and gave her a strong kuuuk of greeting. Used to being her own boss, Bek looked up at the huge white blue heron and merely gave a quick bow of recognition to the Sage. In her thoughts she believed she never wanted to live through the mating experience, let alone relive the experience of nesting that she couldn't chase from her mind. As for the one the Sage had called Mik, she knew that no amount of coaxing would ever bring her within mating distance of the scrawny runt from under the bridge.

The Sage spoke right up. "Now, now, young Bek, I believe thou need to soften thou tenseness. I be aware of what thou lived through in thy birth nest and what thou hath been through since. But I dost believe thy problems be greater than thee think. I be not wanting thee to take offense at what I be telling thee. But I believe thou hath suffered two great traumas which have hurt thee even greater than thy nesting. Again, I wish thou no more hurt. Yet I be reminding thee that thou hath lost two parents and I believe thou be hiding from that grief."

Bek closed her eyes to chase away the memory of those who hatched her. The experience with her aunt and siblings was bad enough. She couldn't handle the thought of the pain she would have to deal with if she allowed thoughts of her parents to slip into her mind. She didn't believe she could live through it. "I know you are the great wise Sage but I will not speak of my parents and I believe you have no right to ask it of me."

The Sage knew he might have trouble with Bek but he had not expected such a robust negative stance. He was offering her a chance not only to save the lake but also to help chase away the intense pain buried deep in her mind. He knew how difficult it was for her to relive her agony, even for such a powerful young bird as herself. The only way he could imagine getting through to Bek was to open up his own heart and allow her to see his own profound pain.

In his rumbling voice the Sage spoke solemnly to Bek. "Listen carefully strong young one, for I be about to tell thee a true tale I have not spoken of for many seasons. It be a tale I think of occasionally because it be part of my life that brought me to now. But it be part of my life I no longer have the need to feel the pain of. Dost thou understand me strong young one? "

Bek looked up into the eyes of the Sage and kuuuked. "I see much sorrow in your eyes, wise white, and I feel that by opening your soul you believe you will be helping me. I'm not sure it is worth your own pain but if you wish to kuuuk, I will listen."

The Sage thanked Bek for her consideration of his hurt but he told her that the story would no longer cause him great sorrow, but it might be of great help to her. He began. "As be said, it be many seasons ago, just before the start of the *Battle of the Dark Marsh*. I be mated to the most beautiful great white heron named Norce. Our love knew no bounds and soon she bore two perfect eggs which we hatched together. One day when I be flying home to feed my family I found my cousin, Greybeard, swallowing my hatchlings, and to make it worse, he had killed my beautiful Norce. As thee can imagine, my grief be overwhelming, but almost instantly it be covered by an even stronger emotion, the necessity for revenge. It was then that I gathered an army and took flight to the Dark Marsh, where the great battle began and ended. That be that it ended but without revenge on my evil cousin, Greybeard.

As I be kuuuking before, thou and Mik's grandparents soothed and healed my damaged body, however, nothing could heal my need for revenge. When I could again fly, I be in search of my foul cousin. I flew round and round the lake with not a sight of his revolting blue feathers. Finally I dropped to the earth from sheer exhaustion. But as soon as my strength returned, I flew to the sky once more to find the fiend who had stolen my love, my reason for being. I be scouring the lake until I be abruptly struck with the facts my own mind had forgotten. I be flying my heart out for revenge when it be in reality that I be flying for the loss I felt for my beloved. The thought of revenge had covered my true emotion, the grief for those I had loved more than life itself.

At that point I be seeing the channel I had followed to the lake where I met Norce. I flew round and round that lake, not looking for my cousin but for my already lost love. It be not long before I spotted another channel and followed it until I came to a great sea. It be so large that even from a great height I could see no land. But I did smell a strange odor and soon realized it be the smell of salt. I cared not. I had lost my love and my will to live.

I flew on over the blue sea, hoping my strength would run short and I be crashing into that water. I be wanting it to take my pain away along with my broken heart. When my strength be at its end I was joyful that my life would soon be over. As I be heading for the deep blue, I saw before me an island. Just a small piece of green with a few small mountains surrounded by forest. I be having no strength left in me but something forced my wings wide and I glided toward an empty beach. I be landing on my belly with salt water washing over my feet and salt water running from my eyes.

I be laying on the beach I know not for how long. Total exhaustion pushed me in and out of consciousness until suddenly my head and beak be splashed with cold fresh water. Startled, I opened one eye and standing over me I be seeing the beak of oldest and most grizzled looking great white heron I could imagine.

Unable to move most of my fatigued body, I opened my beak and kuuuked at him with exhausted anger. "Why didst thou pour life back into this wretched body? Can't thee see it no longer seeks to live?"

The Ancient One answered with indifferent sarcasm. "Well young white, if thou really wanted life's end, why didst thou spread thy wings instead of meeting thou end in the sea? Me thinks thou must be having a greater purpose for thy wretched life."

"I assure you little Beck, there be no answer or vigor left in me and the world turned black once more."

"After some time my strength be returning and my eyes opened to find that I be laying on my back. It be hard to believe that such an old bird be able to turn me over. I soon found the Ancient One behind me. To my astonishment, he had his wings under my wings and he be lifting me to my feet. After I be finding a point of reference, I took one step on the beach and fell straight on my beak. The Ancient One suggested I stay down on the sand while he be fetching more water. I be having no choice but to comply.

One eye be following the Ancient One to a stream flowing off the mountains and into a tidal pool next to the sea. It be not far from where I lay. He quickly returned with a beak full of fresh water and dumped most of it into my beak. The rest he spread over my head to keep me awake. Then he again turned me over and lifted me to my feet. Standing, I attempted to lift my wings but they be unable to move."

Again the Ancient One spoke. "There be much time before thou will fly young white. I be seeing that no food hath entered thy belly for some time. I be helping you up the stream where I be having an encampment and food. It be not many steps away and I shall help thee."

"The Ancient One had been correct, sweet Beck. But I be surprised that his hideaway be covered and close to a small pond fed by the stream. In the pond I be seeing many fish, but wondered why he took so much trouble to keep himself hidden. So I be asking him and he answered."

"I understand young white. From the air it be looking like not much be on this small island. Yet thou wouldst be surprised. In the mountains their be wildcats and other large animals. Besides those, I also be seeing alligators in some of the swamps. Thou cannot be too careful, there always be danger in the world. The trick be to keep *aware* while going on with thou life."

"The Ancient One then used his beak to spear a small fish from the pond and dropped it at my feet. I picked it up and let it slide down my gullet. For the first time since the loss of Norce and my hatchlings, I felt there may still be more to life than agony." Casually the Ancient One spoke up again. "When thou be brought to full health, I be teaching thee some *mindfulness* to help thee ease the terrible traumas I sense life hath put thou through."

"I knew not what mindfulness meant; pretty moorhen, but I sensed only goodness in the Ancient One. He filled me with fresh fish and water and in a few moons I be again able to lift my wings. Although he would not yet allow me to fly, we did take many walks on the deserted beach. The Ancient One told me that once there be numerous great white herons on the island but that be long ago before a terrible plague struck. Most of the great whites died along with his own beloved mate and his hatchlings. I could not help but shed tears for my own lost family and for those of the Ancient One.

He then told me not to shed tears but to always remember the love given by those who be close to thou but hath passed. The Ancient One be saying the whites who be left after the plague be deciding to fly to other islands, but he had kuuuked a loud No. He told them he could never be leaving the place where he be finding such great love. All the whites flew off, save one old great white who said he be many moons too old to make the flight across the sea. He wouldst stay and let his long life be running its course. Before he died, the old one had taught my ancient friend the performance of mindfulness and the Ancient One passed mindfulness, awareness of self in the now, on to me.

Bek, I learned the ways of mindfulness and I have passed the ways on to Mik who be living far across the lake. He be promising to practice the ways until I be believing his mind be cleansed. As for thee, pretty young moorhen, mindfulness shall be passed on to thee, who be starting now."

Unused to being ordered about, Bek stood straight and shouted up at the Sage. "Now! Now you just hold on there, big white! I did not ask for any mindfulness and I don't know if I even want it. Especially if it concerns that runt, Mik. Maybe you should tell me what goes on with this mindfulness stuff, and while you're at it, maybe you should explain why, if you had that beautiful island to live on, why do you not go back!"

The Sage stared down at the small black moorhen somewhat taken aback by her anger and unwillingness to understand the danger moving toward her and the possible destruction of the whole lake. He had explained the problem of Greybeard to the Ancient One who urged him to return to his lake to resist his cousin. He also predicted that there was an even greater threat than Greybeard in the lake, but also to all the fresh waters and to any bird, fish, or plant living nearby. The Ancient One could not see in his great mind exactly what the threat might be. He had said it has not as yet unveiled its true identity.

With the Ancient Ones' words ringing in his head, the Sage had found his way directly home and was now confronted by a small black moorhen who would not listen to reason. If Bek would not cooperate, she could undo all the plans he had imagined to save themselves and likely much more.

Finally the Sage spoke. "Please take a deep breath and soften thy mind, young moorhen. I be not coming to the lake to make thy life worse, but better. Tis true, I could be living a life of comfort on the island, but it would be a life lived for nothing. Thou must think of others as opposed to only thyself. Think of thy older brother, Yaan, whose life thou hath already saved once. Yaan be now mated and they be having four new hatchlings. Didst thee not already put your own life in danger to save his? Thou didst that and now thou must put thy own pain aside in order to save Yaan's family and more. Thou could save the entire lake. So please little one, please allow me to help thee shake thy pain from mind and heart to help thee save all that surrounds thee, all that thou deeply love, even if thou cannot feel that love due to past traumas. For it be those hurts that keeps thee from seeing and feeling the love and beauty that doth surround thee now.

Thou whilst always remember thy pain and suffering because it be part of who thou be. But thee hath suffered enough. Let thee not constantly dwell on painful memories. What happened to thou, happened. Thou cannot be changing what happened. There be no point to beating thyself up still. Thou can be remembering what happened, but thou also must let the pain go and be aware of the love around thee now."

When the Sage fell silent, Bek fell still. She thought of her missing parents. She thought about her uncaring aunt and the overwhelming feeling of attempting to deal with so many young hatchlings. She also thought about her final escape from the nest and then the frightful experience of surviving as a hatchling by herself; alone in the wildness of the lake.

Bek suddenly realized that those memories and those pains were most of what she thought about all her days. She recognized it was the *narrative* of her life and in her mind she was constantly living it over and over. Her only escape from the memories had come from the times she taunted and bullied those moorhens around her. She knew she couldn't live in that dark hole she let herself live in forever. It was not worth it. She had to make a *choice*, and that choice would be the one the Sage had suggested, mindfulness. She understood what he had said. Her memories would always dally somewhere in her mind, but for now she would follow the words of the Sage and learn to be aware of now; live in this instant of time.

Meekly, Bek looked up and spoke to the Sage. "How do I become aware? How do I become mindful?"

ELEVEN
MIK AND BEK MATE

From one full moon to the next, the Sage spent most of his time on either side of the lake teaching both Mik and Bek mindfulness. He taught them how to meditate. When it rained, he taught them to enjoy each drop falling on their feathers and the beautiful feeling which came with each drop. The Sage taught them to live in the moment and not in the past or future, being aware. He taught them physical exercises and how to scan each part of their body for pain and how to resolve it. If they had pain somewhere while exercising he taught them to feel it, how not to chase the pain away but to go into it, to look at it and how to soften it. He taught them to be aware of themselves and the world around them, the *now*.

On the days working with Bek, the Sage noticed the flock of ibis were still grazing on the grassy knoll behind them. He knew the lake and he couldn't remember when he saw a flock of the white, long-beaked birds stay in one place for such a long time. He noticed one bird in particular. The ibis had odd colored grey eyes that always seemed to be watching he and Bek, but he paid little attention. He had much work to attend to and an ibis could cause little harm to neither he nor Bek.

He had also noticed there were times when he would fly north of the bridge to see if anything had changed in the Dark Marsh and thus see what his cousin was up to. He found that whenever he flew over the marsh there was no sign of Greybeard, but he did notice a grey eyed ibis leaving the marsh just as he was arriving. He couldn't help but feel that something strange was going on, but he always had to hurry back to continue Mik and Bek's training.

The lessons had been going well with both moorhens, especially Mik. The Sage had placed Mik in an area with an abundance of food. He was surrounded by reeds and was quite safe. Besides helping Mik calm his nerves with stretching exercises, Mik had begun to grow. His feathers glistened in the sun and covered the scars from previous battles. Mostly, the Sage felt happy as he watched the chip on Mik's wing fall slowly off. It was now time to put Mik and Bek together.

One day when the Sage had finished practicing meditation with Bek, he asked her if she wouldn't like to pay a visit to her brother, Yaan and his mate, Sheen. Bek had already known that Yaan and Sheen had produced their first brood of eggs and now had four hatchlings. Instantly, the thought of hatchlings produced a severe reaction straight through Bek, but because of her mindfulness training she dismissed her intense feelings against hatchlings as something from her past and it did not mean anything now. She agreed to go.

The Sage told Bek that he had something to take care of but would fly to her brother's nest near the Wide Bridge before Bek could bob over there. He did not tell Bek that the thing he had to do was to fly across the lake and ask Mik if he would bob near the Wide Bridge and come just in sight of the nesting moorhens that lived there. Mik still had the memory and scratches he bore from his last encounter with the mating pair near the bridge. He asked the Sage if it was really necessary, and the Sage suggested that he had been stuck away long enough in his little hideaway and it was time for some bobbing exercise. Mik couldn't resist any request from the Sage and finally agreed to meet him near the reeds by the bridge. The Sage kuuuked goodbye to Mik as he flew off and Mik began bobbing towards the bridge.

The Sage reached Yaan and Sheen's nest just ahead of Bek, and kuuuked them pleasantries and informed them that he had invited another guest, a female moorhen who was interested in seeing their hatchlings. He had only just finished speaking when they heard Bek making her way through the reeds.

Surprised, Yaan kuuuked happily to Bek when he recognized his younger sister. They had not kuuuked since the day she had saved his life. Because of what she had done, her reputation as a tough bird was well known around the lake.

Bek did not act like the tough one he expected. She even appeared somewhat shy. Bek kuuuked kindly to her older brother and asked to be introduced to his mate. Bek was introduced to Sheen, who asked Bek if she wouldn't like to see their new hatchlings. Without even a pause, Beck said she would love too and they both made their way to the nest where four quiet hatchlings lay sleeping. Sheen apologized for them being asleep but she told Bek that she and Yaan had just fed them. Bek couldn't help but notice the young ones were thriving and that the nest was well kept with no shells cluttering the floor. Bek even praised Sheen for the good care they were giving their hatchlings. Bek immediately saw the compliment fill Sheen's eyes with pride as they made their way through the reeds and back to Yaan and the Sage.

As they found their way back to the males, Bek looked down the path in the reeds she had made when she had arrived. Bobbing by the opening was a male moorhen she hadn't seen before. She felt an instant attraction to him and pulled the Sage aside to ask him who the new moorhen might be. The Sage looked down at Bek and asked if she would like to meet him. She replied quickly before the new bird paddled away. "Oh yes, he is so big and handsome, I must meet him."

While the Sage led Bek through the reeds to meet Mik, he hid his jubilation. So far his plan had worked. Not only had Mik learned the way of mindfulness but his exercises had placed him in excellent shape. Bek's condition had also improved. She no longer was a young shrew who not only badgered and bullied her peers but also one who would have nothing to do with any male moorhen. Now he hoped the rest of his plan would work out, especially the mating of Mik and Bek.

When the Sage and Bek emerged from the reeds, Mik was but a short distance away. The Sage gave him a wave of his wing, a beckoning for him to bob closer. As soon as he did, he recognized Bek and his back feathers automatically began to roll as a warning when he instantly remembered his last meeting with Bek. Then he promptly relaxed as the training by the Sage took control of his made over mind and body.

To the Sages' surprise, Bek had bobbed straight to Mik, warning feathers and all. In a coy tone she kuuuked to him not to be fearful. She said, "I only meant to welcome a young moorhen I have not as yet seen on the lake."

It was now Mik's turn to be surprised and he looked up to the Sage for help in the situation he had never expected to be in. The Sage spoke up quickly. "Now Bek, I dost believe that thou hath met this handsome young moorhen once before, although it be under different circumstances. At that time the young moorhen had not as yet had time to adjust to the different ways on the south end of the lake. I be very happy to again introduce you to the young stranger. Bek, once again, I be introducing thou to Mik."

Bek's red beak and shield grew even redder when she recognized Mik. Her first thought ran to their violent first encounter and her second was to bob as fast as possible to the closest clump of reeds to hide her shame and embarrassment. But it was her third thought that saved the day. She remembered her training and took a deep breath."Well young Mik, I see you have adjusted well to life on the south side of the lake. While we are close by would you like to meet my brother, Yaan, and his mate Sheen? They have recently started a family with four new hatchlings."

Mik again looked up at the great white with help me again in his eyes. This time the Sage said nothing as he was as astounded as Mik. With only silence coming from above him, the only thing Mik could think of saying to the beautiful female moorhen was a stammering, "Yes, I would love to."

Mik followed the Sage and Bek until they ran into Yaan. At once both male moorhens raised feathers, but instantly the Sage stood directly between each defensive moorhen and cried out. "Hold thy claws young friends, there be no reason for trouble. Yaan, this be Mik from north of the bridge. I know in the recent past there be trouble between thee. That be only a misunderstanding due to Mik's new arrival on this side of the lake. I want thou to kuuuk in friendship. There may be a time in the future when thou will need each other's help. Besides, who be knowing what other relationship may help join thee?"

With the Sage's words, both Mik and Bek peeked at each other with a sparkle in their eyes. After the Sage's speech, Mik and Yaan touched beaks and all was forgiven. Mik was then introduced to Sheen and the whole group traveled back to the nest to kuuuk at the hatchlings. As they all stood around the nest admiring the little hatchlings, Mik and Bek found themselves pushed side by side in the gathering; so close they couldn't help but touch feathers. Instantly, a strong tingle passed between them. They both wished to stand together for the day, but Sheen soon broke up the assembly with the words that the little ones needed to be fed and get some rest. Thus, the small group moved back into the reeds where Yaan announced that he must find food for the hatchlings and the party split up.

When the Sage, Mik and Bek reached the edge of the reeds and lake, the Sage stated that he had much to do and flew off into the sky. For Mik and Bek, there was nothing between them but longing glances and the wish that they could find the words to express their feelings. Finally, as the sun fell below the trees, they were forced to kuuuk goodnight and bob off in opposite directions.

The next morning Mik rose early as there was something he had to accomplish. He skipped his morning meditation and pushed through the thick reeds surrounding his hideaway. As he bobbed through the water, several female moorhens who had refused to even come near him just a full moon ago attempted to interrupt his trip to the opposite side of the lake. Mik didn't even see them. He had a mission.

When he finally reached the small rise on the other shore, he found both Bek and the Sage waiting for him. Both kuuuked him a greeting as he scrambled up the slight hill. Mik wasted no time in stroking the neck of Bek with his own. This time there was no screaming, no dirt in the face, no shoving and no falling into the lake, there were only shiny black feathers rubbed against his neck by Bek.

Their greeting was broken up by the Sage. "It be appearing to me that thou hath been doing much thinking during the moon time. I could be not more happy for thou than I be now. It be my great honor to be the first to see thee together and a greater honor to know thou whilst spend thy lives together as mates."

Mik and Bek's two red beaks rubbed in a lifelong commitment, but none of the three birds saw a grey-eyed ibis take flight from the grassy knoll and head north.

TWELVE
STARTING A FAMILY

After the impromptu mating ceremony, the Sage told Mik and Bek to meet him at a stand of bamboo trees on the far south end of the lake. He had called the trees their Sanctuary as he flew off southward.

Mik and Bek could hardly see the trees because they were so far south across the large lake, although Mik remembered he had gotten a glance of them after he first passed under the Wide Bridge. As both moorhens bobbed across the lake, each stroke of their long yellow legs brought them closer to the Sanctuary. The closer they got, the more excited they became about what they saw.

The bamboo stood on a corner where the lake met a channel about six lengths as wide as the Sage was tall. Thick reeds grew in front of the trees and wrapped themselves around the corner where the lake met the channel. The nearly impenetrable reeds at the base of the bamboo would be perfect place for future hatchlings.

On the other side of the channel Mik and Bek noticed a steep embankment which followed the channel water downstream into a forest. The embankment was about as long as the channel was wide and gradually sloped to a long, flat shore backed by a short, sloping field of weeds. The water in front of the shoreline looked shallow and was sporadically strewn with fauna. Both Mik and Bek realized the flat shoreline just south and east across the channel from the Sanctuary would make a perfect spot to train a fledgling family.

They both were lost in thoughts of their prospects together as they bobbed slowly down the channel. Finally, they were pulled from their reverie by a kuuuk from the Sage. They had been so involved with the vision of their future life together that they hadn't noticed him wading in front the Sanctuary.

"Come hither you two, there be a few things thou must know before thou dost plan a whole new universe." He then kuuuked a laugh which brought laughter to Mik and Bek who heeded his wishes as they squeezed their way through the thick reeds to the Sage.

The first thing the Sage kuuuked was to ask them if they had any problems on their way to the Sanctuary. They both answered no and asked why he should be worried. "I be feeling there be no reason to frighten thee, especially Mik. Thou see there be many more alligators in the south end of the lake. Even though I taught thou both mindfulness, the exercises I taught you must be done each day or thou could easily fall into mind traps from the past. I know what thou have been through Mik, and I be knowing thou hath a particular problem be alligators. Do thou understand what I kuuuk of my mischievous one?"

A short fleck of fear flashed in Mik's eyes at the reminder of his family's demise, but he looked up at the Sage and nodded. Mik did understand and would continue his meditation along with being aware of himself and everything around him in the now.

The Sage spoke again, this time to Bek. "I know thou will be building a nest with Mik. Thou hath had family problems in the past and I also be knowing that past fears will always dwell on thee if though dost not continue the same rituals I have taught Mik. I hope thou will be as faithful to them as I know thou will be to thy mate. Do you comprehend, pretty Bek?" Bek looked up solemnly and nodded to the Sage that she did understand and would follow his instructions.

"Good," the great white kuuuked. Then the Sage continued his introduction to their new home and environment. "As thou can see, there be a good place to build a nest on the open ground between bamboo and the reeds. The bamboo and the reeds grow thick so they should keep thou safe from most predators. But as be stated, alertness be always important for thy safety. In this place there not only be alligators, but snakes, which I know you fear Bek, also turtles, who can pull thou under, marsh falcons who will turn up close to fledgling time, however, most of all thou main concern be Greybeard and his minions. I suspect Greybeard knows thou hath moved south Mik and he may also have spies who might have told him about the mating of thou and Bek. That be the reason I be helping thou to mate. Thou both come from families who be strong. I have seen them in battle with mine own eyes and believe both of thee can defeat any foe, especially Greybeard. But we need more of thou. I be having talks with other birds on the lake and have warned them that I feel war be coming from north of the bridge and we must be ready.

Mik, I be knowing thou be acquainted with Coal. I be speaking to him and he be feeling as I do. He tells me birds of all kind be soon leaving their nests and moving south. Coal be included. Greybeard be inflicting havoc up north and he be dragging that blackness with him. Thou both must help raise and lead an army for all of our protection. Whilst thou be helping?" The young moorhen couple looked at each other with a special glint in their eyes and told the Sage that they would be thrilled to help, especially with filling out the army.

The Sage laughed and thanked the couple and they in turn thanked him. Then he said, "Tis time to leave thou two alone. I have much to do and so do thee." The Sage then lifted his great white wings and rose into the air. Before he was out of earshot he kuuuked to Mik and Bek that they should be fruitful and multiply.

Both birds laughed mischievously at the Sages' sentiments after he was out of sight. Automatically Bek bowed her neck submissively towards Mik who immediately began to preen it. To Mik's surprise, Bek suddenly raised her head and nipped his neck with her beak and sprung quickly into the reeds. Mik didn't wait long to follow, and eventually Mik found Bek floating on the open water of the channel. He hurriedly raised to bite her neck, but when he reached her she dodged him and forced him to bob quicker to catch her. This game went on for some time before Bek finally submitted to their mated commitment.

This exhausting ritual continued for several days until one morning deep in the Sanctuary Bek told Mik it was time for them to begin making an actual nest. Mik understood instinctively what she meant and after the morning meal, they both began gathering broken reeds and sticks. In short order they had enough material for them both to start on the project. They built the nest where the Sage had suggested. It was on the channel shore between the stand of thick bamboo and the even thicker reeds. They would have good protection on all sides and always a close food supply. The nest they built was big enough to hold a large brood of eggs and after that a large brood of hatchlings.

It wasn't long after their nest was finished when Bek announced her first clutch was soon to arrive. She wasn't wrong. A day later, as Mik returned from gathering food, he found Bek happily sitting on a brood of six newly lain eggs. Mik was surprised by the scene. He knew of the problems of her early life but saw her eyes were closed and her slow breathing told him she was in meditation.

Shortly after he had arrived, Bek's eyes opened and she said that she felt wonderful but was hungry and needed to stretch her legs. Mik didn't complain, and as soon as Bek got off the brood he delightedly took her place. It was natural for moorhens to share the incubating of their hatchlings with their mate. He didn't waste any time; when he got settled, he concentrated on his breath and was soon meditating.

It took twenty moons before Bek informed Mik that she had heard cracking in one of their six eggs. By the next moon there were six hatchlings loudly peeping with their mouths wide open for food. Mik quickly gathered seeds from the nearby reeds and fed his family. Then Mik, with the help of Bek, ate every bit of shell strewn on the bottom of the nest. He quickly noticed the practices they had learned from the Sage had taken a good hold of his beautiful mate.

Both Mik and Bek kept up their mindfulness and meditation but by nature they were still moorhens. They still carried with them their cautiousness of the dangers of the lake and its surroundings, especially now that they had hatchlings. Soon their hatchlings would grow into fledglings and their new job would be to teach them to feed themselves and survive in a hostile environment. It wasn't long before the hatchlings had grown enough to start climbing the walls of the nest and Mik and Bek knew their fledgling phase was about to begin.

THIRTEEN
RAISING FLEDGLINGS

Besides trying to climb the walls of the nest, Mik and Bek become aware of their little ones pecking at the nest looking for food. It was time for them to see the world. Mik and Bek both accepted the fact that their responsibilities would grow. Protecting their family in the enclosure of the nest had been one thing, but now their job would be to protect *and* teach them to survive on their own.

While Mik had been out gathering food or just guarding the front of the Sanctuary, he had seen an alligator sunning itself on the flat shore across the channel. On several occasions he had even noticed large turtles sleeping on nearby rocks. Both would think nothing of putting an end to at least some, if not all, of his family. Having claimed the Sanctuary, he and Beck had already chased off other birds that would eat the food supply needed to feed their little ones. Usually it was mottle ducks, but the natural instincts of a moorhen didn't allow any birds to think they could encroach on their territory.

Occasionally he would hear the loud fluttering of the Sage as he flew in to check on their progress, and of course he was always welcome. Mik would kuuuk of the health and wellbeing of his family and the Sage would do the same about life on the lake. The last time Mik had spoken to the Sage the news of the lake had grown worse. Greybeard was eating anything that could fit down his enormous gullet and his territory was still moving further south. To make things worse, his minions, now commanded by Null, were uniting with all other muscovy into one large army with the help of Greybeard. The Sage felt that sooner or later Greybeard's army would attempt to breach the Wide Bridge. The Sage kuuuked to Mik that he agreed with Coal and other birds to have a rotating guard posted on the bridge to give warning of any imminent attack. He also said a small militia was being trained in case of such an attack, and that Bek's brother, Yaan, had volunteered to join that militia. He said he hoped Mik would also join when he and Bek had trained their first batch of fledglings. At the end of their conversation, the Sage quickly took to the sky with a goodbye kuuuk.

Mik felt that the Sage was exaggerating because of the negative feelings he held for his cousin and hoped he hadn't forgotten the lessons he had taught both Bek and himself. At any rate, he felt his only job now was to raise and to protect his family.

Suddenly, a loud kuuuk from the other side of the reeds caught Mik's attention and he wedged himself through the tangled barrier to find Bek leading a file of fledglings along the edge of the water. Behind Bek came Loug, the first of their hatchlings to break through his shell and who

Mik considered his oldest son. Loug appeared to be a natural leader as he followed Bek, and the other fledglings followed him.

Mik was astonished to see that his hatchlings were suddenly fledglings almost overnight. He blurted out to Bek: "They are so young. They just came out of the nest, Bek. How did you get them to walk in a straight line so quickly?"

"They just know how to follow orders, Mischief," Bek answered sarcastically. She saw a partially shameful grin flash across Mik's eyes, kuuuked a laugh at him and then continued. "Help me get their feet wet. They will float naturally and will soon be able to swim in the reeds. In a few moons we'll take them across the channel and teach them to feed themselves. I've already seen them eat insects on the ground as we walked to the water."

Mik and Bek let each fledgling dip their feet into the water, although some were not so pleased. Next they learned to float, and the day after that they could swim through the reeds better than their parents, although their parents wouldn't let them leave the protective cover of the reeds until they had more navigational skills. They still had to learn to swim behind their parents, but it soon became apparent that they had learned the skills necessary to handle the lake. They had now been hatched for six weeks.

Mik and Bek now knew they were ready to bob in deeper water, so Mik peeked through the last of the reeds they had bobbed through for any sign of predators. He saw none and he and Bek led their little ones out into the channel, then a little southeast to the flat shoreline.

It wasn't long after they were on dry land when Bek called Loug to her side. By the time Loug reached her, Bek had already ducked her head under shallow water and had scooped up tiny crayfish with her beak. When Loug reached her, she dropped the tiny creature at his feet. Without hesitation, he reached down, grabbed the offering in his beak and swallowed. Bek put her head under water and found the soft shoot of a new reed and dropped it directly in front of Loug, but almost in the water. She did the same with another tiny mollusk, but this time she dropped it a little further out into the water, Loug rushed out to get it, except this time he was forced to dip his beak almost up to his eyes for his meal. It wasn't long before Loug was putting his head and neck underwater for his food. Before long he was doing it without help from his mother. Soon both Bek and Mik were using the same teaching tool on the other fledglings. In no time all the fledglings were up to their feathers in water, dipping their beaks and necks underwater to gather their own lunch. Finally the lesson ended for the day and the family of stomach=filled moorhens were bobbing back across the channel to the safety of the reeds.

FOURTEEN
TROUBLE ON THE CHANNEL

A few moons after the fledglings had their first self-feeding lesson, Bek held the young birds deep in the reeds by the bamboo Sanctuary while Mik bobbed out in front of the reeds providing security. As he bobbed from the channel to the open lake, he noticed a thin log floating on the water. The log was straight and without branches, except for one which stuck out near the top of the wood. Mik had a fun idea.

He grasped the branch of the log with his claws, floated on his stomach and used his wings to paddle the log into the channel where he stopped close to the reeds. He knew Bek was keeping an eye on the fledglings while they ate from the reeds near the nest. Mik kuuuked for Bek and his son, Loug, to come through the reeds to the open water, which Bek did while the fledglings peeked out at Mik from the outer rows of protective reeds. Without hesitation, Bek chastised Mik for being so foolish. She kuuuked, "How can you be floating around holding a big stick when you are supposed to be watching for predators?"

Mischievous Mik ignored Bek's harsh tone and called for Loug to come from the reeds and into the channel. Cautious because of his mother's mood, Loug sheepishly made his way out of the reeds and bobbed over to Mik, who was still holding the branch of the log with his claws. When Loug got to Mik, he floated aimlessly with no idea of what his father wanted. To his eldest son Mik happily kuuuked, "Come on boy, climb up on the log. I'm going to take you for a ride."

Loug was still not sure about what was going on, but he followed his father's orders and climbed onto the log close to the branch his father held. Before he knew what was happening, his father's wings began paddling through the water and pulling the log along. When his father paddled faster, they were already out on the lake and the exhilaration of the speed and the wind blowing through his thin wings felt like the most exciting thing he had ever felt. Soon he was kuuuking with laughter and hoping the ride would never end.

After a while Mik paddled the log back to the reeds where the whole brood of fledglings floated in the channel waiting for a turn to ride like their older brother. Even Bek couldn't help but float there with a smiling glee in her eyes.

Finally, when Mik grew tired of towing his offspring up the channel, he pulled the log up onto the flat shore not far across from the Sanctuary. All his fledglings followed Bek over to the sandy shore. They surrounded Mik's neck which they all rubbed with their beaks, including Bek who gave him an extra long rub to show her love for him and for the fun he had shown their fledglings.

Suddenly in the midst of the love fest Mik felt a strange feeling in his belly. At first he thought it might be the exhaustion from all his work and then remembered the feeling he felt when he saw his parents and siblings killed by the alligator. With his wings, Mik swept his whole family behind him and searched, first the water and then the sky. Nothing in the water seemed to be unusual but in the sky, he saw the wings of a very large bird heading their way. It only took a moment for Mik to realize that what was coming was a large *wood stork*. He knew the huge bird wasn't coming to kuuuk. It was coming for its lunch and that lunch would be his children.

Looking quickly at the Sanctuary, Mik knew there was no chance his tiny fledglings could swim across the channel before the stork would be on them. His only chance was to push his family back while he walked into the water to take on the huge white threat.

The massive white wood stork, many times Mik's size, landed a short distance before him. The big bird lacked the long neck of the great herons, but it was obvious to Mik that the large bird intended to bend over him and gobble up his little fledgling's one quick gulp at a time. As exhausted as Mik had been just moments ago, a surge of adrenalin flowed through him and his brain screamed loudly, "There'll be no gulping on my watch."

Mik's white feathers had already spread in warning when the stork landed in front of him. The huge bird barely took any notice of the small black bird when he bent his long white body over Mik to begin his meal. Before the big bird's beak was even over Mik's shoulder, an ear shattering screech came from the little moorhen as his feet sent Mik and his shield straight into the stork's stomach just as he was bending over.

The big bird staggered a few steps backwards, but before he had a chance to consider what had caused him such pain, he was hit again. With no time at all to think, the little black bird smashed into him again and the big bird staggered further backwards. He now quickly realized the head of the black bird was down and ready for another charge. He also realized that lunch was not going to be the easy pickings he had first believed and his immense white wings lifted him into the sky in search of easier prey.

When Mik finally realized the threat to his family had abruptly disappeared, his adrenalin rush crashed back to immediate exhaustion and he was barely able to bob himself back to the shore. Let alone fend off his grateful family, who were now climbing all over him and showering him with grateful love.

FIFTEEN

MILITIA TO ARMY

"No!" Yaan screamed at his oldest fledgling. "You have not yet even grown a full red beak or shield. I have spoken over and over about the fact that there *might* be war. You still need time to grow. Otherwise, you will only get in the way, Jowl."

Before Jowl had a chance to counter his father's argument, they both heard a raucous fluttering of wings as the Sage landed beside them. "What be going on here? I could hear thee from the top of the Wide Bridge. Do thou both not know that Sheen is working hard in your nest to keep thy new clutch of hatchlings calm while thee both float in the nearby reeds howling like a pair battling muscovy over a new hen. At least thou could act more civilized than that. Please explain what the problem could be."

Jowl rudely kuuuked before his father could speak. "*He* says I am too young to help defend the Wide Bridge if there is an invasion from the north. I believe I am strong enough to hold my own against any of Greybeard's stinking minions and I want to join the militia!"

Yaan was about to shout back when the Sage set the tip of his great white wing on his back to calm him. "Thou father doth be correct young moorhen. But I be feeling most proud that thou be willing to be putting thyself in harm's way for the good of the lake. I feel thy father must also feel such pride. But thou must understand that for now the best thee can do be to protect thy younger fledglings and thy mother who be struggling with her new hatchlings. It will be some time before the dumb-headed minions of Greybeard will be able to mount any kind of serious attack and I be sure that by then your shield shall be strong enough to bash in the breast of any minion. Dost thou understand my brave Jowl?"

Jowl bowed his head in compliance at the wise words of the Sage who continued. "One more thing strong little moorhen, thy father will not be gone long for his training. I be sure that when he returns, he shall be happy to teach thee all he has learned so thou will be prepared to defend this territory if needed."

The wisdom of the Sage put pride and a happy resolution in the eyes of both father and fledgling. As Yaan made his way through the reeds on his way to the training site, Jowl took a strong protective countenance in defense of his family.

As the Sage took wing toward the north in order to reconnoiter that portion of the lake, he could not help but wonder if what he told the moorhens was true. Null was a much brighter and fiercer muscovy than Goff had been and an attack might come much sooner than expected. Because of those worries, the great white heron didn't notice Zignoid flying swiftly below him in order to warn Greybeard of the Sages' approach.

It took some time for the Sage to fly to the most northern section of the lake, but not as far as it might have been. The heavy black cloud which covered the Dark Marsh had spread wider and further south. Still, he could find no sign of the blue color that would indicate Greybeard. His senses told him not to fly into the dark cloud, so he made a slow turn until he was traveling south once more.

This time the Sage followed the shoreline until he saw a small flock of *wood storks*. The wood storks were mostly white with black under wings. Their thick beaks were bent somewhat downward and their heads were bald, giving them the nickname, *lead heads*. They were stockier than the Sage but their necks were short and ended almost at their shoulders. The Sage thought that if they had a neck and legs as long as his they would be almost be the same height. He had had little contact with the white birds but they were in as much danger as any bird on the lake and with their size they would give his militia an added advantage. The Sage made a quick banking turn and reversed course back to the storks.

The Sage landed a short distance from the storks and all looked up in surprise. He bid them a friendly kuuuk and after some discussion among themselves one bird walked to the Sage. The smaller bird made a friendly sounding greeting the Sage recognized as similar to an Ibis. The Sage raised his tone a few octaves and introduced himself as the Sage.

The white bird with black under wings and a bald head said his name was Skrech and asked what the Sage wanted.

The Sage answered slowly in order that he would be understood. "Skrech, doth thou and thy small flock understand that a great danger be coming in thy direction?"

"No, we see no danger. We like the lake and intend to stay here. So far the only danger any of us have encountered is southward, on the other side of a wide bridge."

In his mind, the Sage was aghast. All the danger he knew about was not too far north of where they stood now. He quickly spoke up. "Hath thou not seen a great blue heron with a grey beard and a flock of evil muscovy north of the bridge? All the danger be here. I be not understanding thou meaning."

"One of my flock, Fleck, flew deep into the south of the lake and stopped for a bite of lunch. He was reaching for a frog when he was attacked by a small black duck-like bird with a red face. Fleck was badly beaten. After the attack he was barely able to fly." Skrech pointed his wing down the shore and continued. "Look for yourself, white Sage. He can only take short steps while walking to his nest and mate. As for the bearded one you speak of, we have seen nothing. But about the muscovy, they gather on the east side of the lake and us on the west. We cannot abide their horrible stink.

My small flock plans to stay here. We have seen nothing of these moorhens nearby. I'm afraid moving south of the bridge would put our future families in great danger. Besides, Fleck and his mate have already built their nest and it contains a brood of four eggs."

The Sage stayed quiet while thinking. He knew Skrech must have been speaking of Fleck having a fracas with a moorhen and most likely, Mik. He understood he must try to remedy the situation and get the wood storks to move south. He finally spoke again. "I be sorry Skrech. There be a great misunderstanding between Fleck and this black bird called a moorhen. Moorhens be naturally nervous and even somewhat vicious. They can be extremely territorial and especially when protecting their young ones. If thou leave them their territorial space they be no problem at all. But I must be reemphasizing that if thou stay north of the bridge, thine whole flock be in grave danger."

"I appreciate your worry for us strangers." But the wood stork's attitude was still adamant. "We have made up our mind in counsel, kind Sage. Nothing but an absolute disaster will change our minds. Again I thank you for the warning but it is here where we shall stay."

The Sage knew what would be coming, but he had said all he could to change Skrech's mind. He bid the small flock of wood storks a kuuuk and flew off to seek out Coal in order to make counsel. The Sage flew south from the wood storks until he came to Coal busily gathering his clan for the move to the south side of the bridge. After failing to convince the wood storks to immigrate south, his heart was low and he hoped Coal would have some good news for him.

Without even a kuuuk, the Sage landed beside the chief limpkin and in an exasperated manner he said languidly. "Tell me thou hath good news for me old friend. My luck be poor this day and my heart be low and needing something to give it a lift."

Surprised by the sudden appearance of his friend, it took a moment for Coal to take his mind off the big move and onto something that would both cheer the Sage and also give him hope that things might be getting a little better. "I have had contact with other birds on the northern lake, cousin. Most seem to understand the imminent danger Greybeard brings with him. All but a few be resigned to move south of the bridge. And, if their words are true, our militia will soon be an army."

SIXTEEN
UNEXPECTED VISITORS

With spirits lifted after hearing of most of the birds willingness to move to the southern end of the lake, the Sage decided to fly further south and pay a visit to Mik and Bek to see how their fledglings were doing. Although he didn't want to aggravate Mik, he must make him comprehend the misunderstanding he had with the wood stork, Fleck. After all, he thought, it be only over a frog.

When the Sage landed near the Sanctuary, Mik and Bek were almost to the flat shoreline across channel. Behind them paddled six fledglings in a solid line. The Sage could not help but notice that the last bird in the line was of a small size, as Mik had been when he was young.

Surprised by the visit, Mik and Bek stood in shallow water and shooed the fledglings behind them. With a few flaps of his huge wings, the Sage was standing before them and a deep friendly kuuuk was coming from his beak. Both moorhens happily kuuuked back to the Sage, not having seen him for some time.

The Sage spoke first in his deep voice. "I be sorry it be such a long time since I last flew by, but much be occurring on the lake and all my time hath been taken up. But I be seeing thou have developed quite a nice family since I be away."

Both parents blushed with pride at the Sage's compliment and asked if he would like to meet them. The Sage kuuuked an excited affirmation and Bek's wing reached behind her in order to lead their oldest fledgling before the Sage. It was now Mik's turn to speak, his voice still filled with pride. "Sage, I introduce you to Loug, the first of our brood to crack his shell." Loug bent his neck with some youthful embarrassment and the fact that the bird before him stood so tall that he couldn't stretch his young neck long enough to politely look into his eyes. Mik, feeling his son's discomfort quickly led him to the rear as Bek filled his space with the second fledgling in line. It didn't take long for the compliments from the Sage to reach the fledglings ears when Bek reached to lead the youngest fledgling who bobbed in front of the Sage while constantly calling out with a loud *peeping* sound. Embarrassed, Bek quickly led her youngest fledgling back behind her and apologized to the Sage for his youngest fledgling's lack of respect.

"Think nothing of it, sweet Bek." The Sage answered quickly. I seem to remember the senior of your family being a bit of a handful when he be young." The Sage gave a wink to Mik and all three adults kuuuked with laughter at Mik's expense.

When the laughter died down Bek announced that the sun was beginning to set and it was time for the little ones to be nested. She thanked the Sage for coming to visit and had already kuuuked goodbye when the Sage asked her to wait.

Bek turned to face him and the Sage spoke with a jovial timbre. "I almost forgot to tell thee, thy brother Yaan and mate Sheen have another nest of hatchlings!" Bek thanked the Sage for the good news and asked him to send her and Mik's best wishes when he sees them again. Then, with the light almost gone, Bek immediately led her line of fledglings across the channel; the youngest peeping all the way.

Mik was about to kuuuk goodnight to his friend and mentor when the Sage stopped him in mid sentence. "I must speak to thee of important matters, moorhen. Let us talk a bit longer." Mik nodded his head in assent.

The Sage lowered his voice and began speaking to Mik. "I be hearing that a moorhen had a confrontation with one of the birds from the new flock of wood storks on the lake. Could that moorhen possibly be thou, Mik?"

Without any feeling of guilt for undertaking his responsibility, Mik spoke up. "Of course it was me. I had no choice but to protect my family." Mik felt some anger at the Sage for asking him about his natural right to protect his own and he said so to the Sage.

The Sage spoke right back. "Calm down, calm down my old friend. There be no blame on thee. Thou be protecting thine own. I be understanding that. But there be some misunderstanding between thou and the wood stork. A wood stork would not be eating a hatchling or fledgling. His beak was only reaching over you to get at a frog for lunch. I have to admit I be somewhat proud to be the mentor of such a small bird who could take on such a large brute. I saw the stork after thou confrontation. He not be in good shape. I be glad it not be me who be in the fracas with thee."

Mik's anger turned to pride with the words of the Sage and he felt larger than his actual size.

The Sage continued his monologue. "Listen to me Mik. Thou understand thy right to protect thou family and territory. Now thou must understand, it be also thou right to protect thy lake and all living around it. For they be thou family too. I be knowing it be only a matter of time before a great danger will befall the south of the lake. Right now Greybeard be gathering an army to attack the Wide Bridge in order to claim the south part of the lake for his own gluttoness purpose. As thou have the responsibility to protect thy family, thou also hath the responsibility to protect the lake thee and thou family live on. Dost thou understand the words I be kuuuking, prized Mik?"

Mik felt troubled but he answered anyway. "I understand your kuuuks, great Sage, but what can a small moorhen like me do against an army of muscovy. There is many more of them than me."

The Sage cut in quickly, "thou be wrong my young mentee. There be many on the lake who whilst join thee. Just this morning I be breaking up a scrap between Yaan who is joining the militia and his eldest son, Jowl, who insists he be old enough to join also. I had to convince Jowl he must take care of his family while his father be away training.

Listen to me Mik. Many more birds be fleeing to the southern lake. They will be standing up to Greybeard and his minions. Even Coal and his clan will be here, along with more limpkin clans that fear Greybeard. What they have missing be a strong leader. I be knowing in your heart and built into your blood be the makings of that great leader. I need thou strength Mik. All of us be needing it."

Mik floated quietly on the smooth water of nightfall. Finally he spoke up. "I understand what your kuuuks mean, wise Sage. But it is much for a small bird like me to take in all at once. I have a family to think of and I must have words with Bek over it. I need some time to think. Do you understand?"

"Of course I do brave moorhen," the Sage said with a sigh. I will leave you now with the beautiful family thou must take care of. But we shall speak of this again soon. Sentries have already seen a few muscovy surveying the Wide Bridge. I kuuuk you goodnight my friend. There be much to prepare."

Mik watched the great wings of the Sage lift him off into the night. Then as he bobbed across the channel to his post by the reeds he noticed one of the ibis who had moved with the same flock on the grassy knoll closer to the Sanctuary. The ibis flew off to the north in the same direction as the Sage. He didn't spend much time thinking about it. He had much more important things to think about now.

As Mik began his patrol in front of the Sanctuary, Bek was busy back near the bamboo getting her fledglings ready to nest for the night. Suddenly she heard a hissing sound coming from somewhere in the bamboo. The sound was familiar from her early embedded memories. Memories which included violent fears but she couldn't remember exactly from where they came. She had learned much from the Sage about how memories could cloud the present and bring back fears from the past. He had also taught that those fears would always be present in her mind but did not have to rule present action.

Bek took several deep breaths and allowed them to seep slowly out her beak. Almost instantly she calmed as her ancient fears slipped from her mind and she continued her nesting duties. As she soothed her fledglings to sleep, the youngest one began his typical peeping. Soon after the peeping noise started, Bek heard a slithering from inside the bamboo thicket and froze in place with the memories of the huge snake that almost devoured her in her early fledgling time. Only now she carried the fears in present time and she knew she and her six fledglings would soon be facing a huge snake with the intent of swallowing them all. At the same time as she recognized the slithering sound she was hearing, she was well aware of the peeping of her little one and the danger his noise was leading to the nest.

Bek could think of nothing to do but shush her baby and try preening his neck in order to throw the hissing predator off their track. It was no use. The more she tried to calm the peeping the louder the tiny fledgling peeped. Bek could see no other way to stop her family from destruction. She had to stop the peeping. She went to the loud little open beaked bird and shoved her own large beak into the fledgling's gaping throat. Instantly the peeping stopped. Bek knew instinctively she had to keep her youngest quiet until she heard the snake slither off in another direction. She listened hard for the slithering or hiss but it had stopped. Almost in hysterics the scent of her brood was not yet on the monsters darting tongue. She held her baby still with her ears listening only for sounds coming from the bamboo. She had no sense of time in her mind, only the feeling of fear. She did not know for how long she felt the stillness around her but eventually she heard the snake zigzag out of the bamboo and slither into the water on the lake side of the Sanctuary.

Bek withdrew her beak from the fledglings and breathed a huge sigh of relief. Suddenly she noticed the peeping below her had not started again. She cried out to her little one but he didn't move. Then she noticed his tiny neck lay still on the floor of the nest. Now she was in full hysterics and the only thing she could do was cry out a violent kuuuk of help to her only mate, Mik.

As soon as Mik heard the terrifying call from his mate he knew there was a horrible problem at the nest. Without further thought he bulled his way through the thick reeds until he found the shore and his trembling mate next to the nest. Below her he instantly spied the lifeless body of his youngest fledgling. The sight stopped him dead in his tracks. At first, all he could do was take in the gruesome scene. Next, he quieted the rest of his wide awake family and finally he did his best to calm his quivering mate.

Bek, he saw, was way beyond hysterics for the death their youngest fledgling. The only word she could manage to blurt out in her frenzied state was "snake." Mik quickly understood the appalling scene in front of him and knowing his youngest sons' habit of peeping, he understood what must have happened.

With the other fledglings under control he gave his entire attention over to his mate and spoke. "This is no fault of yours, Bek. You did what you had to do to protect the rest of the family. He rubbed her neck gently with his beak and led her into a squatting position. While Mik stood over her, he told her to breathe slowly and to be aware only of the space between her eyes. He then began to preen her neck and head and whispered to her to soften her body and sleep.

When he was sure Bek was asleep, he quietly moved to his eldest son, Loug, and told him to stay with the family. He also said he had a terrible errand to run and would return as soon as possible. He then picked up the dead baby by the wing and dragged it through the reeds to the lake. From there he pulled the body to deeper water and as salty tears dropped from his eyes, he let him go. Mik knew other creatures in the lake would take care of his youngest son.

When Mik had finished his dreadful chore he returned to the nest and rested his neck on Bek's. None of the moorhens moved until the next sun rose.

Mik wasted no time. When the sun had risen over the trees he brought food to the fledglings and to Bek, not wanting any to move as yet. Then he searched the embankment across the channel from the Sanctuary. He feared the scent of death might draw more predators that would further endanger his family and a new temporary nest must be established.

Eventually he found a small burrow that had been started but never finished by some strange animal. The burrow in the embankment was already covered by long grasses and most of what he must do was to push the grasses aside and widen the hole. By this time the sun was beginning to set, he again recognized he must work faster to settle his family in the new nest before dark.

After the new nest had its floor packed with soft grass, Mik went back to the main nest, gathered his family and led them back across the channel. The first thing he did was to urge the fledglings into the hollowed out burrow and have them move to its rear. He then had Bek back into the hole with only her red beak showing. He then found more grass to cover the face of his beloved and took to the water where he would float as sentry to protect those he loved even more than life itself.

SEVENTEEN

JULL

Jull ran as fast as possible on his short legs and webbed feet but could not throw off the three young muscovy hens whose beaks clung persistently to his tail feathers. Greybeard had made him the head of his entire muscovy army that repulsive day when he had witnessed his predecessor, Goff, sink into the deadly dark marsh as Greybeard was devouring all of Goff's chicks. Along with control of the minion army, Greybeard had also allotted him all of Goff's hens. Although Jull feared Greybeard down to his bones, he felt elated by the fact that now he not only controlled the largest harem in the huge muscovy flock but also that he would certainly have the pick of any hen in the extremely promiscuous clan.

At first, Jull wallowed in the satisfaction of so many females constantly throwing themselves at him and due to his own ego driven masculinity he didn't put up any struggle against their constant need for pleasuring. His real problem didn't start until the next generation of muscovy hens came of age. As head of the army of minions, all relations to his blood raised the status of any hen that bore his chicks. He was now in constant demand and now satiated to the point that he could barely fight off the number of aggressive hens, like the three who now hung tenaciously on his tail.

To make matters worse, he had recently received orders to appear before Greybeard on a grave matter that could not wait. With the memory of the gurgling Goff still in his mind, he used the last of his strength to shake the three hens from his feathers. Unfortunately for Jull, along with losing the three hens, he also lost three tail feathers.

Although Jull regretted the loss of the feathers, he knew it meant nothing to what he might lose by being late for a summons by Greybeard. Finally, as he reached the water's edge, the black cloud over the marsh caught his eye and shivers of fear ran down his spine. The dread of a face to face with Greybeard and the mob of sex crazed females behind him almost caused Jull to raise to the sky and never return. But with little understanding of the blue heron's magic or how it might be used to torture him, Jull paddled his tired legs directly for Greybeard's lair.

It wasn't long before Jull saw Greybeard standing up to his feathers in the center of the expanded dark marsh. The fact that the large bird stood in the marsh again reminded Jull of Goff and extra shivers of fear shook his body.

Before Jull reached the edge of the black mass, he was already being screamed at by Greybeard who was so angry spittle flew from his beak. "Where in the name of the Dark Marsh have you been you overstuffed soft shelled turtle? Messing with that flock of females I always see you playing with I suppose. When I send for you I mean now, not after you've boffed a few more of your little angels. I hope you remember Goff because you may be him the next time you don't heed my word instantly. Am I understood?"

A mealy mouthed yes Master dribbled from Jull's beak before Greybeard spoke again. "Now listen carefully you stupid oaf. Almost another season has slipped by and few birds for my consumption remain on the north end of the lake. With all the fooling around by your flocks, your army has grown to full size. Am I correct? Dumb one. Don't give me another sniveling answer to that. I have seen it myself.

My spy, *Zigsnot,* or whatever he's called, tells me many of the birds who have flown south have risen a militia of some size. It appears my cousin, Sage, the limpkin clan leader, Coal, and that little runt they call, Mick, are behind it all. I can't have that. My food runs low and we may have to seize the south side of the lake sooner than planned. Understand?"

Another weak yes Master dribbled from Jull's beak and Greybeard continued. "Now, this is what I want you to do. First, send six of your best muscovy males down to the Wide Bridge. Three on each side of the waterway passage under the bridge. Not too close. I want them watching for anything unusual. Keep them in the bushes and wide awake. Two, I want you to begin to mass an army. It must be gathered on both the east and west of the lake for our eventual invasion of the south. Weed out all the weaklings, but keep any females who can fight. Train them to the best of your almost useless ability or at least train them to follow orders. Clear? And third, please find yourself a squad of large male muscovy to protect you from all those lascivious *dillies* hanging themselves all over you. There is no time for fooling around. All your time must go into the invasion of the South. Can you remember that, bald butt?

Oh. One more thing. After you train a squad to protect you from the hens, I want you to expand the squad yourself. Make sure they are the best muscovy you can find. They will have a special mission when the fighting starts."

Greybeard heard one more sniveling, yes Master, from Jull and told him to get his featherless rear back to his flock before he heard his last gurgle.

EIGHTEEN

MIK'S MARAUDERS

Mik and Loug bobbed through the water close to the shore on their way to Yaan and Sheen's territory. A season had past and Loug had grown into a sturdy mature moorhen. He had joined the army soon after Mik gave him permission and proved to be a good soldier.

As father and son bobbed North, Bek was at home tending to a new brood of fledglings with the help of her two female daughters. That is when the two young moorhens weren't out hunting for their own mates.

Unfortunately, Mik and Bek had lost their last male to Ol' Mo as he was crossing the channel. Lucky for Mik and Bek, both parents recovered from their grief with the help of mindfulness, meditation and each other.

Bobbing along, both father and son kept a close lookout for alligators as Mik explained the plan to Loug. "Hear me son. The Sage has described that he has flown many excursions north of the Wide Bridge. On none of them has he been able to catch a glimpse of Greybeard. He *has* seen the minion army and from what it looks like to him the army appears to be in complete disorder. Unfortunately, he has not been able fly close enough to make a proper assessment.

The Sage is also beginning to suspect there might be a spy among us. This is the reason he has planned a reconnoitering mission by you, me, your uncle Yaan and his eldest son, Jowl. We will be much less visible than a huge white bird flying through the sky."

Loug, in his youthful approach, was usually the one to leap into action and ask questions later. Possibly because he knows the plan leads under the bridge, he feels a little more cautious and indicates it to Mik. "But why us father? There are many in the army who are dark and also much bigger and stronger than moorhens."

Mik stopped him and looked directly into the eyes of his oldest. "You are correct my son. We are the smallest, but we are among the bravest. It runs in our bloodline. Our duty is to put the life of the lake ahead of our own. Besides, we are not the only ones involved. Both Duug and Kuun, sons of Coal, hide in the bushes on either end of the bridge. They are keeping their eyes open for us and for any danger they can see north of the bridge. You should feel pride in your heart that we were the ones chosen for such an important mission. It could mean the life of *our* whole lake."

Feeling his son understood, Mik continued with the plan. "We are to travel to Yaan's territory in daylight and wait until the small sliver of moon keeps our lives safe. With our dark feathers and small size we have the best chance of fulfilling this important raid."

Even at his young age Loug now grasped the importance of their assignment. He merely nodded his comprehension to his father. They both turned and silently bobbed on northward.

When they reached Yaan and Sheen's territory they were greeted by both adult moorhens, Jowl, and also the Sage. After the salutations, Sheen went back to the nest to check on her fledglings and the Sage gathered the raiding party for the final briefing on their plan.

The Sage spoke in a whisper to the four moorhens gathered closely around him. "As thee all be knowing, thou whilst be waiting here until the falling darkness. What thou dost not know be what I be recently told by Coal. It be appearing to his sons on the bridge, Duug and Kuun that a party of six large muscovy have taken up positions in the bushes on both sides of the lake just north of the passage under the Wide Bridge. Three on each side."

Mik interrupted the Sage. "It would seem we need an aversion to get past the three guards or our original plan is ruined."

"Thee be correct, Mik," but the Sage continued. "Duug, Coal's oldest, seems to have a workable plan. It be appearing that a single female muscovy has been wandering in the trees above and not far away from the three muscovy observers on the east side of the bridge passageway. Duug be suggesting that both Loug and Jowl doth climb up the hill on this side of the bridge and sneak into the woods. In the meantime, Mik and Yaan shall pass under the bridge close to the east wall. If thou be brushing thy wings against the stone of the passage thou shall not get lost in the blackness and there be less chance of attack by largemouth bass."

Mik interposed again. "But how far should we travel and I don't see a diversion."

The Sage had no problem answering the question. "Duug be coming up with a good plan. Now Mik, thee and Yaan be following the wall to the end of the passage. Thou shall wait there for a signal from Duug up on the bridge. The signal will be three short kuuuk's. The signal means it is safe to bob into the open lake and past the sentries.

In the meantime, Loug and Jowl be stealing their way behind the lone female in the woods. When they are in place, the two young moorhens will rush from behind and scare the female muscovy into the sights of the three male muscovy guards. Thou all know the ways of the muscovy. The three sentries will leave their posts to pursue the female and will most likely fall into a brawl over her. It be at that point where Duug will signal to Mik and Yaan that all be clear and they can rush past the occupied guards and meet up with Loug and Jowl a little further north on the lake. Dost thou all understand or dost thou be having any questions?" The Sage only saw nodded heads from the four moorhens and continued. "Now all thee be needing rest till nightfall, when I will indicate it be time to begin thy venture."

Without even bothering to kuuuk the assembly broke up. The Sage stayed where he was to watch for the moon and nightfall. Yaan and Jowl went to the shore and the nest of their family and Mik and Loug climbed up on shore in search of a comfortable spot to rest until their operation began.

To Mik, it looked as if Loug immediately dropped off to sleep, but he found himself too anxious for slumber. He tried breathing techniques, meditation, even some self hypnosis he had picked up; nothing worked. All he could do was remember his first fearful trip under the bridge and the hope he had felt for life, a new life on the other side. Many joyful things happened to him since he made the move and many regretful things also, but they were in the past and lying sleepless on the bank of the lake, it was now. Before he realized any time had passed, he heard the massive body of the Sage push through the reeds. Before even waiting for the Sages' giant wing to wave, he woke Loug and they both worked through the reeds to their comrades.

Each of the moorhens knew their mission. Without being told, Loug and Jowl began working their way up the slope to the bushes at the end of the bridge and Mik and Yaan pushed through the reeds to the end of the dark passage. Slowly they let their right wings find the slimy stone wall of the passageway to guide them into the blackness ahead.

Loug and Jowl had made their way to the bushes at the east end of the bridge where they met the towering Duug. Without a sound, Duug used his beak to indicate to the moorhens where they could find the female muscovy. The two birds wasted little time moving into the woods where the dumb female muscovy slowly turned in circles having lost her way.

It wasn't long before Loug and Jowl made their way behind the muscovy female. With a predetermined signal given by Loug, the two moorhens suddenly rushed at the muscovy and she ran in fear directly into the sight of the three male muscovy guards. The guards spent no time deciding what to do. All three ran at the female who was too dazed to understand anything except that the male guards were in a terrific brawl to be the one to gain her affection.

From the bushes at the end of the bridge, Duug watched the chaotic scene with his beak ready to burst with laughter. Instead of laughing, he held it in and looked through the bushes down to where the bridge passage ended and saw Mik. Quickly he gave three short kuuuks, meaning all is clear. It was time to move quickly north and meet on the lake up ahead.

When the four moorhens rendezvoused they all stepped up on lily pads for faster movement. They knew the muscovy slept in trees at night, so they had little to fear about being caught. As they moved north, they warned of danger to any birds that might still be on the lake. Most said they would take safety south of the bridge as suggested. All had heard frightening stories of the evil of Greybeard but even with the fear his name dredged up, most of the birds had felt they had nowhere to go.

It was well into the night and Mik thought the scouts were about halfway to the Dark Marsh when they suddenly heard kuuuking. Instantly, Mik raised a wing, the signal for the scouts to freeze in place. The talking was coming from around a bend in the lake not far ahead. As they listened, a slight breeze blew in their faces and the stench told them who they had encountered, muscovy.

It sounded as if they were listening to about five voices. One of the voices was loud and seemed to be in command. The astonishing thing was that they were talking about plans for an attack of the Wide Bridge. Mik and his squad had found exactly what they wanted to know from their raid. The most hopeful words were from the one they assumed was in command. The commanding voice said it was too difficult to train the stupid muscovy and that they wouldn't be ready for an attack until at least the end of the season.

Mik and his crew had stumbled upon exactly the information they had hoped to gather. They had more time to prepare for the attack than they had expected. With the answer they wanted, Mik was anxious to get back to the Sage and pass on the information. He raised his wing again and pointed south. All the moorhens were happy to leave the dreadful end of the lake. With Mik's signal, they all made haste to walk on a lily pad heading back towards the bridge.

Regrettably, when Jowl treaded on the closest lily pad he hadn't seen that it had a slit from the center to the edge. When his weight landed on it he instantly felt he was about to fall. He spread his wings in an attempt to stop a plunge but it was too late. He splashed into the water. In the quiet night air the sound traveled almost to the bridge. Mik also knew it would travel straight to the ears of the muscovy.

Mik immediately waved a wing towards the west where a small island stood in the center of the lake. As quietly as possible they slid into the water and bobbed with all their strength towards the island.

As they bobbed quickly through the water, they could hear a commotion on the lakeshore and Mik thought he heard the name Greybeard mentioned. When they pushed themselves through the reeds surrounding the island they climbed onto land and the small squad of marauders turned to see if the muscovy followed. None had; their commander had been correct, muscovy were hard to train. The moorhens took advantage of their lack of discipline. They followed Mik across the spit of land, climbed into the water and bobbed calmly west behind Mik. The leader of the marauders was clever enough to keep his squad between the island and the muscovy.

Unluckily, the muscovy weren't the only ones on the north end of the lake. The splash had reached Greybeard's lair and into his sleeping ears. His eyes automatically flew open but he saw no danger. He figured the distant splash must be that of a falling coconut or maybe a jumping fish. The thought of a jumping fish caused an abrupt pang of hunger to erupt in his stomach. He felt the urge for an immediate snack and remembered the small flock of wood storks on the west side of the lake. Just that day he had flown over the storks after lunch and had noticed a nest of hatchlings. They were exactly what he needed now. Greybeard lifted his wings and flew to the west side of the lake in search of the nest.

Unaware, Mik's marauders landed exactly on the west of the lake where the wood storks nested. The first stork to awakened was Fleck, who had a family to protect. Next came the leader, Skrech, who awakened the rest of the flock. All the wood storks knew the small black birds with red faces were a threat and took up defensive positions.

Before Mik could explain they meant no harm and that the fracas he had had with Fleck had been a misunderstanding, Greybeard himself landed directly between the two groups. All three parties were astonished.

The moorhens were the first to put up their warning feathers. The white storks kept their defensive positions because Sage had already warned them of Greybeard. Once over the shock of having his little black enemy right before him, the great blue stood still.

Greybeard didn't stay still for long. When the situation finally came into focus, his long neck and beak shot out in the direction of the moorhens. His beak was met with nothing but air as the moorhens had swiftly changed position. The great blue pulled back his neck for another strike, but before he could, Jowl rammed his shield directly into his empty stomach. The blow jolted Greybeard and he fell back a few steps.

The four marauders knew they were no match for the huge blue heron, but the bash by Jowl gave them seconds to form a plan. Mik was about to speak but Jowl spoke first. "It was I who was responsible for our plight. I chose the wrong lily pad and splashed into the water. It is I who will hold off the evil one while the rest of you bob for the bridge. I will abide no decent. I do this for my family, my lake, and our freedom." Without another word, Jowl ran at Greybeard and smashed his stomach again.

The three other moorhens looked at each other with the understanding that Jowl was correct. They all knew there was no chance for them to beat Greybeard and their news had to reach the Sage. With dreadful fear for Jowl, yet also swelling with pride for their courageous comrade, the three moorhens watched Jowl hit Greybeard one more time. Then they instantly turned and bobbed rapidly for the bridge.

Greybeard saw the moorhens flee out of the corner of his eye but he still needed to contend with this pugnacious black bird before him. Greybeard took a step back into the water and struck again at the moorhen and missed again. Jowl quickly made another run at the blue but this time the blue was ready. Greybeard stepped aside and struck the moorhen in the wing with his beak. The tremendous size of the great blue knocked Jowl on his side, but not out. He rolled completely over and made still another run at the blue. This time Jowl was not so lucky. Greybeard had maneuvered himself to be over the small moorhen and his beak pierced straight through to Jowl's heart. He died without a kuuuk.

By the time Greybeard looked up for the other three enemies, their feathers had blended into the darkness and they were gone. At that point he didn't much care. He had taken quite a beating from the tiny black moorhen and his gate was unsteady. The only thing that felt steady was his hunger. He stumbled directly through the line of white storks to Fleck's nest. Without a second thought, Greybeard rapidly gobbled down the four peeping hatchlings. Next, the horrified storks watched him as he slowly hobbled down the shoreline and disappeared into the blackness of night.

The three surviving marauders bobbed swiftly past the three muscovy sentinels who were caught looking the other way and swept into the blackness under the Wide Bridge. Their right wings again guided them through the tunnel until they exited the other end and stopped to rest and wait for Jowl.

The three survivors waited until sunrise when it was silently understood that the fourth marauder hadn't made it. The first thing Mik and Loug did when that realization struck was to surround Yaan with sympathy for his loss and for the incredible courage shown by his son, Jowl. He had saved them all. Slowly the three small moorhens bobbed back to the reeds where the grief struck father must tell his mate that their oldest son was gone.

Mik and Loug let Yaan enter the reeds first to deliver the awful news to Sheen while they took their time to locate the Sage to give him the good news. When they located the Sage and told him about the fact that they wouldn't be attacked until at least the end of the season, his spirits seemed to zoom. however, when they told him of the loss of Jowl, he crashed. Neither father nor son could find the words to console their beloved mentor. They both understood it must be even harder for what Yaan and Sheen must be going through at that same moment.

None of the three could kuuuk for a long time. Finally the silence was broken by the deep voice of the Sage. "There be no words I couldst kuuuk that could diminish our pain. I whilst not even try. All I be saying is how much your sacrifice and of course, Yaan's, means to the lake. We now be having time to put together a good plan. I thank thee again, Mik and Loug.

I believe thou be needing a good rest now and it be good for you to bob for home. I shall spend some time with Yaan and Sheen in order to commiserate and attempt to heal some of their grief. After that, I must fly east to confer with the Ancient One about what must be done next."

The Sage then kuuuked goodbye to Mick and Loug and headed into the reeds to meet with Yaan and Sheen.

Having nothing left to say, father and son bobbed slowly south on the long trip to again feel the love and warmth of their own family.

NINETEEN
COURAGEOUS MIK

Mik didn't return home to the warmth and love he had expected. For one thing, he returned home alone. While traveling south, Loug met a small flock of female moorhens. Loug told Mik he would meet him at the Sanctuary if he didn't find a female who was attracted and enthralled by his recent raid exploits. When Mik finally reached the Sanctuary, he pushed his way through the reeds and was confronted by a nest less full than when he left and the tear swollen eyes of Bek.

Bek was afraid to tell Mik what had happened. She was aware of the problems he had as a fledgling. She was happy he had made it home safely, especially when Mik preened her neck as a sign of his love. That act alone allowed her to open up to her mate even though she knew of his past and she hoped the shock would not cause him pain.

Bek's beak didn't want to move, but finally she slowly began her sad tale. "Yesterday, when I took our fledglings across the channel to teach them feeding under water, we were attacked by an alligator on the shore. I tried to fight him off but he was so big. Nothing I did put an end to his assault. I thought he was after me but suddenly he turned and ate two of our young ones. Oh, I'm so sorry," Bek cried. "There was nothing I could do." Tears again leaked from her eyes but she continued. "We stayed on the shore until I believed the monster was gone. Then I led the rest of the fledglings back here. We've been hiding in the nest since then."

Mik stopped preening and stood in a frozen stare. All the fear he felt at the loss of his own family rushed through his brain until he saw a picture of the Sage. The image of the Sage helped him understand he had to deal with the grief that was now. Tears rushed to his own eyes and his black neck leaned on Bek. At least this time he had a loved one to share his grief. They cried together for a long time.

When all their emotions had leaked from both of them, the noise of their remaining fledglings caused them both to realize they still had responsibilities. Mik told Bek he would travel through the reeds to see if any alligators were in sight, then they would take their hungry fledglings out for food. Bek agreed with the plan and Mik, still wracked in emotional pain, slowly made his way through the tangled reeds.

Mik finally reached the last row of reeds and peeked through for any sign of alligators. He saw none, but what he did see across the channel were a trio of *American coots* who were eating by the shore in *his* territory. The overwhelming grief he felt in his heart turned to anger and he rushed from the reeds head down directly at the coots. American coots were a bit larger than he but with the same black feathers although, their beaks and shields were white.

American coots can fly, which all three did when the saw Mik's red beak and shield aimed directly at them. Satisfied that they had left, Mik turned back to the Sanctuary to inform Bek that no alligators were in sight. Just as he reached the reeds he heard a noise and turned to see double the number of coots eating his family's food. He made another rush at this group, but instead of flying off, they split into two parties. Mik could only handle one group, which he did and chased them off. When that group flew away Mik turned to the other trio and found that there were even more of the white faces. He rushed at that group but they only moved aside as he charged through the center.

By this time Bek had heard the angry kuuuking of her mate and went to the edge of the reeds still worried about alligators. When her red beak pushed through the last of the reeds, she found Mik madly charging in circles, attempting to hold their territory. It only took Bek a glance to assess the situation and join Mik in the fray. With two moorhens in the fight, the coots were slightly more wary. Each red face was able to take on the whites until another of the flock of coots flew in and landed in the center of the ruckus. As hard as Mik and Bek tried, they were by now completely outnumbered and exhausted. Still, more coots arrived and the exhaustion won.

Mik and Bek now had no choice but to admit their defeat and head back to the nest. Once huddled with their remaining fledglings there was nothing to do but listen to the ravishing of their food supply and wait.

Eventually the food frenzy ended and Mik and Bek listened as the white faced coots flew their stuffed bellies off to settle in the large lake.

As soon as the other birds were definitely gone, Mik squeezed through the reeds and looked out on the channel. It was empty and Mik assumed it was safe to cross the channel. He kuuuked to his family to come out and follow him across the channel with the hope that some leftover food would be found.

Mik had been mistaken. He and the family had only just begun to peck at any food left by the coots when suddenly a huge alligator lumbered up on the shore not more than a few wings away from Mik's family. All of a sudden Mik's adrenalin went hyper. He felt he had let his family down once already that day and it wasn't about to happen again.

The first thing Mik did was to screech a warning kuuuk to his family, then rush screaming at the giant intruder. The alligator took no heed of the small black moorhen and opened his tooth filled maw with the hope that the bird would jump in as his lunch. It didn't happen. Mik was so hyped up and angry that he jumped straight through the open jaws. The alligator was now between Mik and his family, and that was exactly what Mik wanted. He screeched at the alligator to get his attention and he kept on screeching as he made short quick lunges at the monster. At each advance the gator tried to grab Mik in his wide mouth but he was too slow. Mik would jump back and screech more loudly until the gator's ears could stand no more. Slowly the alligator turned to the water, crawled in, and submerged to quiet the hideous noise of the screeching little black bird. Soon the alligator swam off and Mik huddled on the shore surrounded once again by his loving family.

When Mik's strength returned and they were sure the gator was gone. Mik and Bek cautiously led their family back across the channel and into the Sanctuary. As they squeezed through the reeds they all ate a beaks full of ripe seeds. With their hunger finally satisfied, Bek led the fledglings back to the Security of the nest while Mik casually bobbed along the reeds on his routine sentry duty.

TWENTY

MIK TAKES COMMAND

Within a few moons Mik noticed that the white faced coots always stayed off shore and he had seen no signs of alligators. Soon the family was back to its typical routine across the channel on the flat shore. Loug had taken a mate and already had a brood of eggs. The next two oldest of their four fledglings had grown close to maturity. Mik and Bek felt secure enough to let them begin short forays onto the lake alone. It wouldn't be long before their trips would turn into searches for mates. Mik wondered how the moons had passed so fast.

One afternoon Mik's sentry duty was interrupted by the kuuuk of the limpkin leader, Coal. Mik watched the large brown bird land in the shallows not far from the Sanctuary. Mik kuuuked a greeting in return to his friend and bobbed over to hear of any new news from around the lake.

The closer Mik drew to Coal the more he realized that anxiety filled the body of the big bird. When Mik reached him he had to ask, "What is the problem, Coal? You appear to be out of sorts. Is there anything I can help with?"

Coal spoke quickly and earnestly. "There is much you can help me with Mik. My sons, Duug and Kuun, have spotted movement of Greybeard's minions. They are gathering on the east and west side of the lake. From their perches on the bridge my sons saw that the muscovy are only a short distance north of the island you traversed during your raid earlier in the season."

Coal had kuuuked so fast; Mik had a hard time understanding him. "Calm yourself, Coal. Because the muscovy have moved their camps does not mean that an invasion is imminent. The season is not yet near completion."

Still excited, Coal continued. "I know there is still more time until the season ends, but maybe the minions of Greybeard got special instructions from their Master since you last heard their commander kuuuk. Besides, the Sage has been gone for almost two full moons, and nothing has been heard from him. Maybe he is lost or even dead. How can we protect ourselves without his wisdom?"

Mik understood why Coal was so anxious. The birds on the entire south end of the lake had come to depend on the Sage. "I'm sure the Sage is well. He is able to take care of himself. He knows danger is coming and will surely be home soon."

Coal answered with a slight quiver still in his voice, but he was somewhat calmer. "What if he does not? How will we protect ourselves? Who will lead?"

Mik thought hard but had no answer for his friend. Finally he kuuuked. "You can lead Coal. You were in the Battle of the Dark Marsh. You have experience in war, and your clans have grown since the marsh battle."

The large Limpkin lowered his head in a countenance Mik thought was shame. "I hate to admit it brave moorhen but I am getting older. In the time of the Battle of the Dark Marsh I was young and my blood ran strong with anger and thoughts of revenge. The muscovy Greybeard sends at us may not be the smartest ducks but many are young and they follow any order given by the great blue heron. That is even to death. No, there is no way I could gather the strength to command an army against such an enemy.

I must kuuuk the truth I know, Mik. It is you who are the one. It is you who raised himself to maturity. It is you who bobbed his way to freedom alone under the Wide Bridge. It is you who led the raid on the north. It is you who chased away the tooth filled slithering monster in order to save his family. What is more, it is you who has the courage to command and train the army we have built."

Mik was taken aback by the powerful words spoken by Coal. Inside, he did not feel full of courage. He fought off the alligator only to protect his family. He fled south of the bridge because the Sage urged him. He could not be the one in charge of the defense of the south. He needed time to think it over and he needed to kuuuk with Bek. That was the only answer he could give Coal at the time. "Please dear friend, I understand the plight we face. But I do not believe I am the one you kuuuk of. I am only a lowly moorhen who tries to care for his family. It is possible that I am the one you seek but I must kuuuk of it with my mate. I cannot give you an answer at this time. However, if you will come to me after tonight's moon passes, you will get my answer.

In the meantime, you need to send more of your flock up on the bridge. We must know all the movements of the muscovy. You also must travel to the nesting area of the wood storks. They are in grave danger from the muscovy if they haven't already smelled them. It is you, my limpkin friend, that we depend on now. My true answer will have to come later."

"Are you hearing yourself, courageous moorhen? You already are sounding like the leader we need." Then Coal kuuuked goodbye and he flew off back toward his gathering clans.

When Coal was out of Mik's sight, he pushed through the reeds in order to kuuuk with Bek about what he should do.

Bek was surprised to see Mik come through the reeds much earlier than usual. The expression in his eyes gave her pause and she instinctively knew something serious was about. Even before Mik reached the nest she sent her fledglings to play in the reeds. Mik had something important to kuuuk about.

With a questioning look in her eyes, Bek kuuuked, "What is the problem Mik? You look so troubled. I heard you kuuuking with Coal but I couldn't hear what was kuuuked, but he sounded anxious. Is everything all right on the lake?"

Mik kept his feelings as even as possible. "Coal's sons have told him they saw large encampments of muscovy on either side of the north lake just above where I crossed that small island during the raid. He feels they may attack the bridge before we suspected. He feels that I should command the army we have amassed until the Sage returns. Most of his anxiety comes from the fact that he fears the Sage may not return at all."

Bek thought deeply before she kuuuked. Mik had grown tremendously since she first watched a tiny runt come from under the bridge. While thinking about it, she realized there wasn't even a comparison since those days. They had learned so much from the Sage since then and they had had three broods of fledglings. Some had already gone off and started their own nests. Mik had shown courage in many ways she never thought a small wading bird such as a moorhen was even capable of. But she also knew if there was an invasion from the north it had to be repulsed and at this point there was no great Sage to help stop it. She held fear for the lake but most of all for her mate.

Finally she kuuuked, "Why is Coal not taking command of the military. He has had experience in war?"

Mik gave the same excuse as Coal. "He said he is too old to take on such a task and I believe him. He is not the same bird I met on the shore long ago. Time has taken a toll on his body. He has asked me to take command. I was not sure how to answer and held that I must kuuuk with you first. He is coming by tomorrow to hear my answer."

Bek thought hard and kuuuked again. "Do you have doubts about your ability, because I do not? You are by far the strongest and most courageous moorhen I have ever met. Yes, I am afraid for you, but I am also afraid for the lake, our young ones and all the birds for that matter. You have trained with the army. You went north to the enemies own encampment. I have even heard on the lake that before he left, the Sage spoke to Bob, the chief of the small flock of *osprey* who fish here. They intend to help along with the few *great white egrets*. I also heard the white-faced coots and the mottled ducks will help. You could also depend on any single female and you already know they can be tough. You have a bigger army than you know."

Mik began to look for excuses to turn down the command. "What about Loug. He now has a mate and clutch of eggs. Who would take care of them?"

Bek kuuuked quickly. "I would help of course, but we still have two fledglings that are not yet mature. They would also help. I believe it is your duty to take command, Mik.

I know you. You would rather stay on a straight path like on the straight Wide Bridge. Have another clutch of eggs so you will have fledglings to tow around the lake with the tree branch. Didn't the Sage teach you about the Zig Zag Bridge he saw many lakes away? The bridge turns left and right and right and left but eventually gets you to the other side. Right now you must take another turn on the zig or zag on the bridge of life. You have no choice but to accept the zig, come up with a new plan that will still get you to the other side of the bridge. Right now your choice could mean life of death for this whole lake and all creatures in or around it. Do you understand, Mik?"

Bek's faith and pride in Mik made up his mind but all he could do was to nod his head in acceptance of her kuuuks. He then bent his head low for Beck to preen its top. They both felt their love, joy, and acceptance of his new path as the commander of the South Bird Army.

TWENTY ONE
RETURN TO ISLAND

After Mik's raid, he had kuuuked that no attack should be expected until at least season's end. The Sage made a quick decision to visit his friend, the Ancient One, far to the east on the island in the Salt Sea. Besides his need to visit the Ancient One, the Sage wanted to seek his help about what he should do about the trouble on his lake, especially Greybeard.

The Sage recognized the flight would be long but not as long as his first journey, which almost ended his life. As he was leaving the island, the Ancient One had given him directions that took him straight to his lake, which made the flight much shorter. Still, he knew he had to fly a long distance.

When the Sage finally reached the island he flew directly to the Ancient One's encampment. To his dismay, the old great white was nowhere to be found. Besides not finding the Ancient One, his encampment was in complete disarray and all the fish in his small pond were gone.

Fearing for his friends life, the Sage began a hunt of the jungle in widening circles while he kuuuked his name. Finally, exhausted from his flight and fearing for the old great white's life, the Sage felt the last of his strength give out, along with the will to keep searching. He made one last call from where he stood just as tears began to fill his eyes.

Completely done in, the Sage stood watching his tears splash to the ground, when to his surprise he heard a weak kuuuk come from some low bushes not far off. He knew who it must be and summoning the last of his strength he hurried to the undergrowth where he had heard the sound. Hope now filled his heart. When he pushed aside the low bushes with his clawed foot, hope almost fell in a heap on the jungle floor. The Ancient One was obviously in terrible pain and almost unrecognizable. The Sage tried to stem more tears but found it impossible until he heard the old white croak a faint, "Sage?"

The Sage again used his large feet to crush all the bushes surrounding the Ancient One. When his mentor was completely uncovered, the Sage realized he was even in worse shape than he had first thought. He was so thin the Sage couldn't understand why his feathers hadn't fallen out. One wing was bent in an odd shape beneath him and the Sage realized immediately it was broken. The Ancient One tried to speak but the Sage told him to be quiet and still while he got him some fresh water.

The Sage took one more look at his friend, and then crashed through the jungle to the Ancient One's encampment. As his beak scooped what little water was left in the pond, he noticed one of the small stones making up the dam which held back the stream had been knocked out. Without a second thought he used his foot to shove it back into place, and then rushed back with a beak full of water to his badly injured friend.

When the Sage reached the Ancient One he was making an attempt to move but the Sage put a wing softly on his chest to indicate he should be still. Then the Sage opened his beak and allowed a little water to dribble into the beak of the Ancient One. Next, he dosed the old one's face with the rest of the water and ran back for another supply.

The Sage reached the pond again to find the repaired dam had already caused the water to begin rising. He even noticed a small fish swimming in the pond. The sight of the fish lifted the great white heron's spirits. He thought maybe things might be getting better. He may even have reached the island in time to save the Ancient One's life. The Sage didn't ponder the idea for long as he scooped more water and hastened back to his injured white.

Upon reaching the Ancient One, the Sage's spirits sagged again. He found the old one kuuuking in an unintelligible murmur and what body parts would move, he was trying to thrash about. The Sage dribbled more water in his beak and more was splashed on his face. Putting a wing on his chest again stopped the twitching but the Sage knew he must do something about the broken wing to help relieve the Ancient One's pain.

Standing over the withered old white, tears almost started falling again as the Sage felt so helpless. Finally, he remembered some of techniques his mentor had taught him and began using them. First, he took in a deep breath, held it shortly and allowed it to slowly release through his nostrils. While using the technique he concentrated only on his breath. He repeated the breathing a number of times, then fell back to his breaths natural rhythm. Next, he kept his mind concentrating only on the space between his eyes while emptying his mind and thinking of nothing. He wasn't sure how long he stayed in the meditative state but when he loosened his body he found his mind cleared of frustration and anxiety and now looked again at his old friend and knew what must be done.

Looking down at the old white again, the Sage noticed the neck was twisted in an uncomfortable position and he felt lifting his head and neck might be a good place to start. Before he did anything, he trampled down more small brush to give him more working space. Then he gathered as many fallen palm branches as possible and placed them behind the Ancient One's head. Then, while standing behind him, the Sage carefully lifted the old one's head and neck with both his wings as gently as possible. While he held the neck and head slightly in the air, he used one leg to push the palm leaves under them. He then gradually lowered the head and neck. So far he hadn't heard a whimper from the Ancient One and assumed he might be unconscious.

Once the Ancient One's head and neck were up and straight the Sage noticed that his shoulders had lifted somewhat also and his own wings could slide under the shoulders and lift the decimated old bird. He tried it and found that the Ancient One weighed next to nothing. With that knowledge, he decided to try to lift a little more and it worked. He knew next would be the hard part. While the Sage held up the Ancient

One, he had to reach down with his beak and pull the broken wing from underneath his friend's back. That was where the trouble would begin.

The Sage took several more calming breaths and reached for the broken wing. He had barely moved it when a horrible screeching kuuuk flew from the old bird's beak. Fortunately, he fell unconscious again and the Sage was able to remove the trapped wing from under the Ancient One. He then placed it gently by his side. Quickly, the Sage ran back to the pond for more water.

When the Sage returned to the Ancient One with his beak full of water, he found him lying comfortably in the same place. Unable to speak with his beak full he merely stood looking at his mentor, who kuuuked right up. "Don't thee just stand there gawking young white. Swallow that water. It be looking like thee be the one dying."

The Sage swallowed the water but stood awhile looking at the one who should be dead, giving him orders. Still aghast, he finally spoke up. "How could thou be so chipper when only a short while ago thee seemed almost dead thyself?"

"Thou be still a silly thing, young white. Dost thou think thee be the only bird on this island that be knowing mindfulness?"

The Sage still stood in bewilderment over the vitality that seemed to come back into the old bird, especially in the condition the Sage had found him.

"Be not so surprised young white. I be knowing that my long life be having only a short time to breathe. But I thank thee much for making it more comfortable and for being with me for the last of it."

Still astonished at the Ancient One's seeming recovery, the Sage had to kuuuk him. "How can thou kuuuk of your last days? A short while ago thou be on death's last step and now thee be already chastising me. Thou be still having many seasons to go."

"Hath the water in your beak moved to thy ears young white?" The Ancient One kuuuked. "Doth thou be thinking I know not when my time be coming? And doth thou not know I be happily waiting for that to happen?"

The Sage was not pleased about the direction the conversation was turning and changed it. "Tell me Ancient One, what be causing thee to fall into such retched circumstances? I be finding the encampment to be almost completely destroyed."

"It be a long sad tale young white. But if thee returns to the encampment and brings me more water, I be telling thee." Immediately the Sage headed for the encampment, but was stopped by the Ancient One. "While thou be at it young white, take another gulp of water for thyself. Thou be looking worse than I be feeling."

Shaking his head, the Sage continued through the jungle. He found it astounding that the old one could still kuuuk such cynicism after what he must have been through. Excited to hear the story he rushed to the rising pond took a gulp of water and then filled his beak with more for the Ancient One. He then hurriedly returned to his friend, anxious to hear his tale.

When the Sage reached the Ancient One he found him in meditation mode and waited for him to finish. When he did, the Sage dropped more water in his beak and stood silently to hear what had destroyed the camp and almost his old friend.

The Ancient One choked down his beak of water, cleared his long throat and began to kuuuk his narrative. "I be losing track of time but a number of moons ago, I be opening my eyes to a beautiful sunrise. As be usual, I did my breathing exercises, scanned my body for any new or old friendly pain which might have crept into my joints and completed my usual meditation. After my meditation, I felt a strange feeling of being watched but thought nothing serious about it. I be spying a fat fish in my pond and speared it for breakfast. As I be feeling the fish wriggle down my gullet I be hearing in the bushes an odd rustling sound. When you be coming to the island for the first time, young white, I be telling you of the mountains and wild cats. Fear suddenly be striking me that one might be in the bushes. I be right. He sprang viciously at me before my old wings could be lifting me to flight.

Fortunately I be able to wrestle from his sharp claws and run into the jungle. I soon be knowing the cat be hungry and wasn't giving up his prey. I be hearing him coming through the jungle and again I tried to lift my wings for flight but he had injured me badly. I couldn't fly. Luckily

I be noticing a tree nearby that I could pull myself up on with my beak and claws.

Unfortunately, I be a little bit too late. The big cat be seeing me climb the tree and jumped for me. His sharp claw caught my leg and he almost be pulling me back to the ground. He then lost his grip as I be climbing even higher where I be finding a strong branch to settle on.

The cat be not giving up easily. He be climbing the tree himself but I be too high for him to reach. Eventually, he climbed back down and walked around the tree growling and screeching. This be going on most of the day until he lay down beneath the tree and slept. I could not be sleeping.

It be morning when I hear him go to my camp, splash in the water for fish and tear up anything that smelled of me. He returned to the tree. Another sleepless night for me. Next morning, he be still under me. He still went to the camp to eat fish and be doing this for moons until one morning he be gone.

I be listening for the cat until the sun reaches the top of the sky. Finally, I be feeling it safe to climb down but it not be easy. I be tired and weak. I could feel my leg was badly damaged and when I be putting weight on it I be falling from the tree, into these bushes and onto my wing. At once I knew my wing be broken and it be trapped under my back. I be finding no way to lift my weight off my wing. At that point, I be ready to say goodbye to my life. That be until a few moons later when I hear a friendly kuuuk coming to me through the jungle."

Standing in astonishment over the old one's broken body the Sage had to ask, "How could thou be surviving so long with such painful injuries? Especially when thou knew no help be coming."

"Silly young white, doth thou be listening to me when I be teaching thee the power of now and mindfulness? Of course I be scanning my body with my mind for sources of pain. Where I found them I be not shying away. I be feeling them, concentrating on them and softening them until they flee. Besides, I be knowing thee be coming since thou be leaving your lake and be flying here."

"But how be thee know I be coming?"

"Ancient One be not just my name, young white. I be living and learning for too many seasons to count. I be feeling thou and thy lake problems since we be first meeting. Thou must know we all be subconsciously connected, including earth and skies. Another thing I know be questions thou need answered about the troubles on thy lake."

The Sage pondered what the Ancient One had kuuuked and finally came to the conclusion that he was correct. All be *one*. "I be understanding the meaning of what thou kuuuked old one. What can thou be telling me of the problems on my lake?"

"I know I be not having another moon left, Sage. Hence me answer be quick. Thy suspicions of a spy be correct. He be hidden in a flock of birds and answers only to thy cousin, Greybeard. He be easy to discover with his deep grey eyes.

"How be my cousin be controlling him?"

"Greybeard be having him captured by his minions. When they brought him before thy cousin, Greybeard had them pluck a grey feather from his beard and thrust it into his nostril.

The problem with thee cousin be not all his fault, although he be allowing it to occur. He be in league with an evil b*lack menace* which I be observing a small number of times in my long life. I be not able to advise thee on ridding the lake of it. As I be not able to see beyond now. But I be having great confidence that thou and thy cohorts, the two black moorhens, be working it out. But I be adding that the black menace cannot live in water that be of salt."

"Ancient One, I be understanding thee about the problems on my lake. But what be the meaning of thou not having another moon left?"

"I be joyful to be kuuuking that I be standing on the edge of this lifetime, young white."

Again, the Sage was astounded by the Ancient One's answer and kuuuked his disbelief.

The Ancient One slowly lifted his good wing and kuuuked the sound of *shush* to the Sage and begun his explanation. "I be happy standing on the edge of death because I know when I step over that edge I be having a chance to look back on my life and see what I did, good or bad. I be choosing what needs to be fixed in another life before I be returning to the great nothing that be all that be. From the seed of *nothingness* I be cracking from an egg to begin again a better life from what I learned from this one. This be leading me further to my eternal *salvation*." On the word salvation the Ancient One kuuuked to the Sage, his head fell over, and he died.

The Sage stood helpless as he watched the Ancient One's life escape from his broken body. Swiftly, many tears fell on his clawed feet. Knowing nothing else to do, the Sage automatically fell back to his knowledge of mindfulness and meditated again until he did know what to do.

What to do was for him to use his sharp claws to dig a shallow hole next to his friend. Use his beak to drag the Ancient One's shriveled body into it. Claw back the loose dirt over him. Spread palm fronds over the loose dirt and roll coconuts onto the pile to hold it in place. Then he returned to the encampment, ate a few of the fish that had swam into the pond, drank some water, lifted his wings, and began the heavy hearted long journey back to his lake.

TWENTY TWO
THE PLAN

When the Sage finally saw the mainland below him he decided to find a quiet spot to rest, eat, and grieve. He knew from Mik's raid the war would not start until the end of the season. So he found a small swamp surrounded by jungle and assumed in the water must live fish. They did and except for a few small fish from the great whites' pond, he had his first full meal since leaving his lake. He spent several extra days resting, meditating, and contemplating what he had learned from his departed mentor, the Ancient One.

While the Sage was relaxing, Jull, the leader of the minion army was extremely aggravated as he hurried to a conference with his second in command, Nub. Not hiding his anger, he told Nub that their Master had pushed up the time of their invasion of the south by a full half cycle of the moon. Nub immediately complained that the army was not yet ready for such an undertaking, but Jull told Nub to try telling that to Greybeard. Nub shut his beak and Jull continued. "The Master said he had word from his spy that the Sage has not been seen recently. The rumors on the lake are that he has left on a trip far to the east. Greybeard feels the time to attack is now, when there is no bird to command the south's small army. I tried to explain that even with our army outnumbering the south by twice the size, we have not trained our muscovy well enough yet. His answer to me was an emphatic, *win now or don't come back*. At this point Nub, we have no choice but to attack as the Great Blue has ordered, and we must win."

Jull knew his army was not made up of the smartest birds on the lake and he wished he had more time for training, but he didn't. He had his orders and Jull feared disobeying Greybeard more than he feared for his life. He had watched Goff's agonizing death and he knew his might be even worse.

Adding to the problems of handling an undisciplined army, it also included single females. They were much smaller than the males but could put up a ferocious fight when threatened or in a contest over a male. Jull had tried to explain to his master that allowing females had already led to many fights and injuries. But Greybeard had insisted the size of the army was more important. A large one might scare off the southern birds before any conflict even began. Jull had begun to protest further but the look in Greybeard's eyes forced his beak shut. Now he must explain his battle plans to Nub who was only a little larger and only a bit smarter than the rest of the army. He also had deepening questions about Nub's courage. The only saving grace to the plan was that he did have a large squadron of commandos he had viciously trained himself.

Jull began explaining what he wanted from Nub, but he did it speaking simply and slowly. "Listen to me carefully Nub; this is what I want you to do. I want you to fly to the west of the lake where your army waits. I will lead the army on the east. Greybeard had said he has flown high over the south lake and it appears that the birds there have made little preparation for war. He has seen some limpkin sentries on the bridge and some training going on in the open fields west of the south section of the lake. We will have some element of surprise due to our earlier attack than planned. Plus we have a much larger army."

"What shall I do if our troops begin fighting or frolicking, Jull?"

"Just take some of your largest and most disciplined males and tell them they will be rewarded with extra hens if they beat any muscovy caught fooling around or fighting. However, tell the enforcers not to injure any of them badly as we will need them later. That is what I have already done with the army on the east and it has worked fairly well so far. Any more questions, Nub?"

"No, I believe I know some muscovy males I can count on to keep order. Continue with your plan, Jull."

Jull had doubts about how much command Nub actually had over the western army but at this point he had no choice but to trust him to follow his plan, so he began. "To begin with Nub, we have two armies, one on either side of the lake. I believe the enemy will consider us as split and try to take advantage by fighting one of our armies at a time. That is how I would plan the battle if I were them."

"Me too chief," Nub broke in. "That's what I'd think."

Jull ignored his subordinate's disruption or just plain brown tailing and continued. "I want you to hold the west army in place until I can have a squad of commandos fly onto the bridge to kill or chase off the limpkin sentries. Do you understand so far, Nub?"

"Yes sir, commander." Nub gave Jull a small winged and uncalled for salute before he continued. "I hold my army in place until I see muscovy controlling the top of the bridge."

"Good Nub, you've got it so far. Now, when you see us in control of the bridge, I want you to begin marching your army to the edge of where the waterway continues under the bridge. Be sure all the males have their red erectile feathers on their heads raised. I want them to look as fierce as possible. Understand?"

"Yes, march to the bridge, erectile feathers up. I got it."

"Good Nub. Now I want you to wait for my signal. That's when I clap my wings three times. You won't be able to hear it. But keep an eye on me because you will see it. Then we all charge under the bridge in mass and annihilate any bird on the south side. Get it?"

"Yes commander, I get it." Nub threw another quick salute to Jull. "But why do we not all fly over the bridge? You know us muscovy have not much oil in our feathers, so swimming is not our strong suit."

"You are not listening, sub-commander. For one thing, if we fly over the bridge there is a good chance we could lose control of the army due to maneuverability. We have had no chance to practice any flying tactics.

The other thing is that by flying, they will see us and we will lose any chance of surprise. If our entire army pours out from under the wide bridge at once, we are sure to overwhelm any resistance the enemy can put up. That will be our surprise. They will believe we shall fly over and will have prepared for that. Streaming our whole army under the bridge means we will overwhelm them with our mass of muscovy. Nothing can stop us. Now do you understand?"

Nub gave another quick salute to Jull and flew off to spread the plan to his army. As he flew off, he left Jull shaking his head. He wasn't really sure if Nub understood any of his plans.

TWENTY THREE
THE WEST ARMY

When Nub landed back with his western army he quickly explained Jull's plans to his five largest and most trusted muscovy, especially his main henchman, Crou. Along with the war plan he instructed them on Jull's order to thrash any bird in the army they caught fighting or fooling around. The word of not fooling around passed quicker through the army than did Jull's war plans and understood less.

While Nub waited for the plans and his order of no cavorting in the ranks to be passed through his army, he stood patiently watching Jull's army march to the passage leading under the Wide Bridge. He feared the idea of swimming into the darkness under the bridge but had been more afraid to mention it to his superior. He had told Jull that swimming wasn't the best idea, but that suggestion had reached deaf ears. After not getting anywhere about swimming, he had quickly given in to all of Jull's plans. He feared too many questions would cause a loss of confidence by the commanding muscovy and he might be replaced if Greybeard had any second thoughts about him.

A sudden commotion on the bridge ahead of him brought Nub's thoughts back to the present and he looked up to see many muscovy commandos land on the center of the bridge. He saw Jull's commandos split, one group going east and the other west. Both groups fought the tall limpkins that were putting up a fight but slowly retreated. His heart felt happy about the fact that this war may be over quicker than they had thought and he was also happy about the many hens added to his harem for his part in what was sure to be a great victory.

When he saw the last of the limpkins being driven from both sides of the bridge, Nub wasted no time marching his troops down the west side of the lake to take up their position next to the dark watery passageway. Then he stood waiting to see the three claps of Jull's wings, meaning it was time to charge. Suddenly, he heard a huge uproar going on behind him and was forced to take his eyes off Jull to see what was going on.

All Nub could see behind him was a storm of feathers flying in all directions. Luckily a gust of wind blew many of the feathers away and he could make out a large disheveled muscovy pushing his way through a mass of muscovy bodies toward him. His first fear was that they had been outflanking by the enemy and his life might be in danger.

As the large muscovy moved closer, Nub recognized his chief henchman, Crou. When Crou finally fought his way through the turmoil to Nub, he knew he would hear the real reason for the pandemonium. Before Crou could speak, he was forced to cough a mass of feathers from his beak. Nub spoke first. "Speak up bird! What in the name of the Dark

Marsh is going on? I have a war to win and I can't move my army until whatever this hubbub is, stops."

Still catching his breath, Crou finally answered. "Sir. The order you gave for males to raise their red erectile feathers when we got to the bridge caused a frenzy. When the males complied with your order the females went wild. It appeared to them as a signal for copulation and any female who couldn't find a male fought another female for a chance at a male. Before I could do anything, the males were fighting over who would have their way with any female. Sir, the west side of the lake is covered with fallen muscovy and another body bobbing in victory over it. What can we do?"

Nub looked across the water and saw Jull looking back. It was too far to see his face but he knew it wouldn't hold a happy look. "Crou, find all the male muscovy in reasonable condition and beat every bird in the army who is on their back or bobbing over another. We must get this army standing again. Jull must be furious and if his plans are not followed, he could report us to Greybeard and who knows what our fate might be."

"Sir, it will take some time. I don't know how much but I will try my best. Also, I hate to be the bearer of more bad news but some muscovy are already dead. I doubt there will be much fight left in *them*."

"You stupid mud worm! Just do the best you can, but do it fast. We're in a war, whether you know it or not. Gather your men and start swinging. Otherwise, it will be you who gets swung at. Now move!"

After Crou disappeared back into the feathers again, there was nothing Nub could do but turn to Jull and shrug his wings.

It took until the sun was overhead for Nub to reform his army. When he and his henchmen had finally pulled it together, Nub caught the eye of Jull and pointed one wing under the bridge meaning he was ready. Finally Jull clapped his wings three times, which meant, *Charge!*

TWENTY FOUR
THE DEFENSE

The Sage had not yet returned to the lake, and with the urging of both Coal and his beloved mate, Bek, Mik had no choice but to take over command of the southern army.

Mik had already trained with most of the army, especially the new ones who had fled south of the bridge in order to escape Greybeard. All of the moorhens now lived in the south, along with all the limpkin clans, the mottled ducks and the ibis. Finally the wood storks had arrived.

After Greybeard had eaten Fleck's chicks, their leader, Skrech, had taken his flock and made a hasty retreat south. After Skrech met with the moorhen commander, Mik, he realized Mik was a reasonable bird. He then came to an understanding about what had happened between Mik and Fleck. Immediately, he and his flock joined ranks with the southern army.

Mik was pleased to have the small flock of storks on his side. They were large and strong. If he needed to, he knew he could count on them to take to the top of the bridge and roll rubble down on the muscovy, and that might be happening soon. As the sun began to rise that morning, a large army of muscovy had reached the east side of the passage under the bridge and another army was ready to march south from the west side of the lake. Mik had guessed that when the two armies reached the Wide Bridge they would fly over it or swim through the dark tunnel under the bridge in order to attack the south end of the lake. Whichever strategy they used worried Mik. There were twice as many muscovy in the northern army than his birds in the south.

The Sage had warned Mik before he flew east that the first thing the muscovy would probably do was to take over the high ground. In this case, that meant taking over the Wide Bridge. The Sage had told him that Jull, the commander of Greybeard's minions, would probably send a large squad of specially-trained muscovy commandos to take over the upper bridge before the war ensued. That would give Jull the advantage of overseeing the entre war.

Mik had immediately seen the Sage's point and was happy to now have the strong angry storks. What he didn't have was the Sage. Mik knew only one thing he could count on to figure out how to use the storks and command an Army; his own wits. Mik had to plan two defenses. One strategy if the muscovy flew over the bridge and one if they went under.

His first strategy was the easiest to deal with. If the minion army flew over the bridge he had already decided to spread his army out and fight the smelly muscovy where they landed. His reasoning was that when the minions took to the air they would scatter and have no solid formation. None of the southern birds, including the Sage, had seen any of the muscovy practicing flying tactics. They might even be blown off course by a strong wind and not even reach the southern end of the lake. That's what Mik hoped.

His other idea was much harder to execute and his moorhens had only a short time to learn to fight in a wedge. If the northern army came under the bridge in mass, they would overcome whatever strategy he could imagine. Sure he thought, the long legged birds would wade into the waterway on either side of the passageway and their sharp beaks could do lots of damage, but the majority of the muscovy would make it straight through and overwhelm any floating birds in their way. That's where he had come up with the idea of the wedge. If three or four V-shaped wedges could set up solidly in front of the passage, they could split up the oncoming army and the reserves behind the wedges and the wading birds on the sides of the passage would even the odds against his outnumbered army.

His only problem was that the only practice they had with the wedge was on dry ground. The minion army was attacking much sooner than expected and the maneuver had never been tried on the lake. If necessary, they would have to take their chances, and Mik hoped the front row of the wedge would lift their claws at the same time. To be sure the maneuver was timed perfectly; Mik would command the front wedge. He told the front line of moorhens to follow what he did.

Mik didn't have much time to think more of his two strategies. The minions were already at the east side of the passageway. If the Sage was correct, which he usually was, Mik thought he had better get his army ready for either plan, now.

The first thing he did was to order Coal to fly up to the top of the Wide Bridge and explain to the sentries that if they were attacked by muscovy, that they were to put up a weak fight and slowly retreat into the bushes and woods at the end of the bridge. He then went to Skrech and told him to split up his flock and hide in the woods on each side of the bridge. They were to wait there in case a squad of muscovy commandos chased the limpkins off the bridge. Then, when they received a signal from Coal, both limpkins and storks were to attack the minions and drive them off the bridge. Also, if it were possible and they had the time, the wood storks were to push any rubble they could move on the bridge to the edge. When the actual war began, it would be their job to push the rubble onto the minion army, that was if the muscovy chose the passage under the bridge. At once, both leaders obeyed Mick's orders.

Mik went back to formulating his strategy until he heard a disturbance on the bridge. It seemed to Mik that he had just given the orders to Coal and Skrech, but he wasn't paying attention to time. He glanced up at the bridge and from his angle on the practice field to the west of the bridge passageway, he saw a large squad of big muscovy land in the center of the bridge. At once the large ducks split their squad and began attacking the limpkins on the east and west of the bridge. The limpkins were fighting back but also slowly retreating to the brush and woods behind them.

After the muscovy commandos had driven all the limpkins off the Wide Bridge, they gathered in the center of the bridge cheering their victory with a loud puffing from their beaks and a whooshing sound as they swung their wing. This form of a winning celebration went on while the leader of the commandos leaned over the edge of the bridge and signaled that his mission was over and had been a great success. Without more ado, the entire east muscovy army joined in with the puffing and whooshing in unison with the commandos. The noise was so loud it was heard on the entire lake.

When some on the south side of the lake heard the incredible sound they froze in fear. That was until they heard an equally loud kuuuking scream coming from the bushes and woods on both sides of the bridge. Instantly following the sound, two large units of both limpkins and wood storks charged from their hidden positions on either side of the bridge. The battle that ensued on the center of the bridge was devastating. Both the limpkins and the storks had good reason to hate the muscovy; their evil connection to Greybeard.

As for the muscovy, they were taken by complete surprise. The well trained commandos put up a valiant fight but the hate and need for vengeance by their enemies overwhelmed their training.

The ruinous effect of the short skirmish on the bridge was ghastly for the commandos. The tall limpkins and their pointed beaks and the shorter but sturdier storks showed no mercy to the minions. The muscovy were knocked to the ground and their heads crushed by the claws of the limpkins. Some limpkins just shoved their beaks directly through the eyes of the muscovy. Other storks barreled into their enemy and thrust them roughly over the side of the bridge. Before long, all the commandos had been killed or pushed off the bridge. The battle was so quick and brutal that none of the southern army were even injured.

Abruptly, the east muscovy army went silent and the silence on the whole lake was deafening. But the silence didn't last long. Suddenly, from the west side of the north lake grew a ferocious sound. A sound that was never heard by any bird on the lake and louder than the muscovy victory ritual.

TWENTY FIVE
THE WAR

Upon hearing the staggering sound coming from the northwest side of the lake, both Coal and Skrech rushed to look over the edge of the bridge. What they saw and heard automatically forced their wings to cover their ears. If it were possible, they would have also covered their eyes. Below them from the bridge to far down the west lakeside they saw an army-size cacophony of screeching, cavorting, bobbing, wings swinging, hitting and muscovy feathers swirling over half the northern lake. Both birds looked at each other in awe.

When Coal and Skrech got over their shock, Coal attempted to kuuuk over the uproar coming from below. Finally, Coal removed a wing from his ear and waved to Skrech to follow him across the Wide Bridge. When they reached the other side he kuuuked as loud as possible to Skrech. "It looks like Jull and his sub-commander have on their wings quite a serious situation." Skrech didn't try to answer; he just rolled his eyes in comprehension. "It appears the sub-commander will be using a fair amount of time to pull his army back together. It should be buying Mik extra time to get his defenses in sync; especially now that it be obvious that the muscovy army be planning to attack the south from under the bridge. Here's what I will do. I am going to divide my limpkins and send half to each side of the southern passageway. We cannot swim and fight, but we can wade in deep and spear any muscovy coming from under the bridge." Still kuuuking loudly, Coal continued. "Here's what I think the storks should do. I see that you are strong enough to hold the bridge against the muscovy. I also see much rubble your storks can roll to the edge of the bridge on both sides, and when the muscovy come, instruct them to push the rubble onto the muscovy. I believe that is Mik's plan." In agreement, Skrech nodded his head. "I am splitting my limpkins now. Then I will fly down to Mik to explain what is happening. Do you agree?" Skrech nodded once more. Coal then instructed his limpkins on the plan and flew down to confer with the commander.

Mik had watched the short skirmish on the bridge and was not only surprised but astonished by its ferocity; especially by the limpkins. He had always felt they were big, but timid birds. The brutal exception by both limpkins and storks began to give him hope that they could win against the larger army.

Coal soon landed by Mik's side and explained the melee taking place on the west side of the Wide Bridge. Coal assured Mik of the fact that he had more time to prepare than originally thought. He was also emphatic that the muscovy army would definitely be attacking by swimming under the bridge. He had seen the muscovy preparing to take to the water when they regained control their western army.

The news that the muscovy would be advancing from under the Wide Bridge gave Mik another idea. He quickly summoned both Yaan and Loug. When his son and brother-in-law reached him, he described a new twist to his original plan. "Listen carefully moorhens. I heard from Coal that the muscovy army will definitely swim under the bridge when they strike. Yaan and you, Loug, have already been under the bridge and you know how dark it is." They both nodded. "The minions will be swimming blind and a large squad of dark moorhens under the center of the passageway will never be seen. Can you see what I'm getting at?" Both Yaan and Loug looked at each other, and then shook their heads, no. Mik explained further. "Can't you see? A large squad of black moorhens won't be seen. When the muscovy reach your point in the center of the bridge you will be free to raise your claws and attack. This surprise assault could throw the entire muscovy army into confusion. It may even force more muscovy to the sides of the passageway and give our wading birds many more targets. Now do you understand?" Both birds nodded that they understood, but they wore a worried countenance on their faces. "Look, I know it sounds like a suicide mission. But done right, you and your fellow moorhens could come out unscathed. The muscovy won't be able to see you and if you bob out from under the bridge, the muscovy will be blinded by the sun's bright light."

Yaan spoke up quickly. "Yes, the muscovy will be blinded, but so will we. What will protect us then?"

"Don't worry, Yaan. I will explain to our defense force that you will be mixed with the invading army. They will watch for you and kuuuk loudly so you can avoid the clawed wedges. Besides, I will be the lead of the first wedge and will keep an eye out for you. Don't be afraid."

Loug was the next to speak. "I am not afraid, father. I trust your judgment and I have seen your courage against many enemies larger than you. All I can say is that there are so many of them. How many do you think I can kill?"

Mik couldn't help but kuuuk a laugh at his oldest son's bravado and rubbed his neck with his own while putting a soothing wing around Yaan. "You are my bravest moorhens and whatever happens, it might be that bravery which gives us a chance to win this war. Now pick out a large squad to follow you both, but pick no moorhens I am training for the wedges. I can't spare any who have already been trained. Now hurry, we may not have much time."

In the time it took Mik to get back to wedge-training he saw Yaan, Loug and a good size squad of moorhens bobbing into the blackness under the bridge. He silently wished them well, especially his son Loug. He knew in his heart their mission was extremely dangerous. Then he began kuuuking orders to his wedge teams.

Mik had hoped he could get enough moorhen volunteers for at least three wedge teams. Moorhens by nature were solitary birds other than with mates and family. To his surprise he got many more recruits than needed.

He had picked the largest moorhens for the three teams, but even on dry land they had been difficult to train. Now Mik had to lead the three wedge teams into the water for the first time. He wasn't sure what their land training would turn into then.

Since he was in command, he had figured on being the leader of the center of the three teams. He had chosen two leaders for the other two wedges; one male and the other female. The triangular wedges would have ten on each side and ten making up the rear. He had tried to add up the amount of moorhens but it took the help of Coal to count the number of moorhens in each wedge. It was fifty-five. Both sexes were included in the wedges. Mik knew quite well, any female could be as fierce as any male when it came to protecting territory, maybe even more so.

His plan for using the wedges was simple in his mind, but following through was not easy. On land he had taught the first two flanks to float with claws up and if one was knocked out of commission, the closest moorhen to him or her would fill in the gap. If the three wedges worked, they could split the invading army in four confused groups. He had only a vague idea about the size of the northern army but by the sightings of Coal, it was large.

He had the advantage of the wood storks on the bridge pushing rubble onto the muscovy. He had his secret force under the bridge. He had the wading birds in the water to attack any muscovy near the passageway opening. Hopefully, his wedges would split the main force of muscovy into four groups. Mik had a good number of reserves to attack what was left of the northern army.

His backup forces were made up of all the floating birds Mik could muster. Most of the moorhens had come south and all the males and any of the females not caring for broods of eggs, hatchlings, or fledglings had joined. Surprising to Mik, the white-faced coots had also joined, along with the mottled ducks he had teased so ruthlessly. Also surprisingly, a small force of *anhinga* had volunteered. The anhinga were fairly large and swam long distances under water. They would attack the muscovy as his submarine force.

If Mik's strategy worked as planned, once the entire army of Greybeard had run the wedge gauntlet, the wedges would turn and enter the fray by attacking the muscovy rear flanks. He knew he had a solid plan, but he could only hope it would work. He would soon find out as he led his three wedges into the water for its only chance for wet training.

At first, the wet training went awful. His moorhens were confused by the light waves on the water and they found it hard to discover which wedge they belonged to. Soon, they all fell into a panic mode and bobbed for dry ground. Mik didn't panic. By force of will he stopped their rout and led them all to the center of the bridge, about twelve blue heron wings length from the bridge itself. He then gathered his other two leaders and kuuuked to all the wedge birds to circle around their particular leader. When the wedge troops were finally in three groups, Mik and the other leaders then led their groups to their designated positions in front of the passageway opening and began forming their three wedges. It wasn't easy on the water but eventually it was accomplished; and none too soon. Unexpectedly, the raucous racket coming from the other side of the bridge fell silent. The next sound they heard coming from under the bridge was an earsplitting echoing word. *Charge!*

Mik knew what was coming; the army of Greybeard's minions. Although to his bewilderment, no bird had seen a glimpse of the remorseless Greybeard, but it bothered Mik not a bit. He had much more to worry about now, not about himself, but about his son and Yaan and their squad who would feel the first brunt of the assault.

Mik couldn't see them but he knew instinctively that already the wood storks were pushing rubble onto the muscovy charging under the bridge. The debris they had pushed together and off the edge couldn't miss. The muscovy army was so massive there was no space between the large ducks. Each projectile raining on them damaged and sometimes killed a muscovy. A loud kuuuking cheer reached Mik's ears with each hit. He knew he wouldn't hear cheers from under the bridge but the ferocious charge must be reaching Yaan and Loug's squad of disrupters about now.

Mik was correct. The thunderous sound and nauseous smell of the muscovy reached the squad before the muscovy themselves. Under the enclosed passage, retching would have been in order but for the discipline installed by their leaders. They had already been trained to breathe through just their mouth and no upchucking came from any of the squad. They merely spread out, lifted their claws and took the massive charge claws on.

The front line of the muscovy was the first to hit the claws and each member of the squad tore up their opponent who had no idea what they were up against, but the muscovy ranks did somewhat split. Yaan and Loug had already planned for that and the entire squad of moorhens lowered their beaks to the water and slammed outward in any direction. They couldn't miss a muscovy body. The damage they conferred on the enemy was enormous. Although the push of the large army behind didn't slow, the enemy kept coming. Now Mik's plan began to work. A natural sense of terror forced the large army into confusion. Comrades smashed into their comrades. Some crushed the birds in front of them, some turned back to be driven under water, and some smashed into the sides of the passageway. In a horrible death, some drowned.

Yaan and Loug couldn't help from being dragged along the passageway as if they were caught in a rushing river. They couldn't be seen and the confusion they caused left damaged and drowned muscovy all though out a large swath of the army. Soon light began to fill the blackness under the bridge and the sound and smell of the waves of the ducks reached Mik. Almost instantly they poured from the depths of the passage and were blinded by the bright sun, but the push from the army behind them wouldn't allow them to stop.

Mik only had an instant before he caught a glimpse of Yaan and Loug. Fortunately, they were being driven along with the group of muscovy who went between the wedges. Other of the moorhen squad weren't so lucky. Some were injured or killed by rubble pushed from above. Some were swept into the risen claws of their brother moorhens, ripped by the claws, and then crushed under-water by the following army.

Mik's own wedge held together tightly. They clawed many of the enemy, although the large mass of muscovy did push them backward. Still,

Mik's plan was working. The muscovy army split into four large groups which spread confusedly around the northern section of the south lake.

The wedge on the right of Mik wasn't so lucky. They had managed to cope with the first wave of muscovy but were overwhelmed by the second line of enemy. Eventually the wedge came apart and most were overcome by the enemies' numbers. The wedge on Mik's left performed better. They had lost a number of moorhens and were no longer in a triangular shape but they were still a working faction.

Suddenly, Mik noticed a severe scuffle going on above him on the bridge. Jull had landed a large contingent of commandos to take back the bridge. To him it looked like the storks would have trouble winning. Mik managed to catch Coal's eye and pointed his wing up to the bridge. Coal immediately understood and ordered his limpkins back to the bridge.

After Mik had signaled Coal, **he noticed a single large muscovy taking his time** as he swam out from under the watery passageway. He also noticed a quick motion on top of the bridge. Instantly, he recognized it as Fleck, the stork who he had had a conflict with and the one whose fledglings had been eaten by Greybeard. Without a moment's hesitation the stork jumped feet first off the bridge and landed directly on the back of the lone muscovy. The muscovy was driven straight down under the water along with Fleck. Both of them drowned. Later, Mik learned that the drowned muscovy was the cowardly sub-commander of the northern army, Nub.

Mik only had an instant to feel his heart breaking for the courageous stork before he began gathering all his wedges together. He divided them into four squads and sent them to attack the enemies' rear flank, who were already engaged in a fierce battle with his reserve defense.

Although already tired from their first confrontation with the muscovy army, the reformed wedges slammed straight into the rear of the invading muscovy. The force of their hit took the minions of Greybeard off guard and confused them even further. However, there was still a large number of muscovy and they turned to fight the moorhens that were now floating claws up. The moorhen flanking maneuver had taken the muscovy by surprise and some of their numbers were swimming away or trying to fly off.

Regrettably, it wasn't going as well for Mik's reserve force. Even though disorder had been driven into the ranks of the muscovy they were still a powerful force and the reserve had had little, if any, training. Numerous moorhens had collided with and been run over by the larger muscovy. The mottled ducks had it worse; they had no combat experience and were crushed or easily scared into flight by the northern army. The anhinga were faring somewhat better. They were able to attack from below and bite or pull the muscovy underwater. Unfortunately, there weren't many of them and after each attack they were forced to dry their wings.

Suddenly, Mik's eyes caught a frightening sight. Both Bek and one of his single daughters were in combat with two big muscovy. They were holding their own, but it didn't stop a strike of fear for his family from surging through his body. Even though they were putting up a good fight, the whole reserve force was being pushed back almost to the southern edge of the lake. To Mik, it looked as if winning the war was falling into doubt.

The southern army were fighting for their lives and home so the battle continued. With little time to spare, Mik turned and glanced at the bridge. At least there it appeared that the storks and limpkins were on the winning side of that battle, but when he turned back he saw his own daughter being tossed into the air by the two muscovy. His whole body now went red and he ferociously slammed into any muscovy in sight. However, his fury wasn't winning the war. He knew in his heart it was almost over and they were about to lose everything.

Unexpectedly, Mik heard a screech from the sky. The whole battlefield became still and looked up. Screaming down on the unsuspecting muscovy came Bob and four other *ospreys*. Behind them followed three *great white egrets*. The muscovy never knew what hit them. Meteoric speed and the osprey's claws, along with razor sharp beaks of the egrets tore them to pieces. The southern defense forces, seeing the carnage caused by their flying friend's, kuuuked fiercely with a renewed sense of hope, and along with the kuuuk came a wild counter attack on their hated enemy.

Mik's hope soared, but at the same time he saw Jull coming straight at him with hate filled eyes. Mik just managed to bob out of his way and turn back with beak in water. He hit Jull with a glancing blow that threw him to his side. Mik then came directly at him, claws raised. He barely caught Jull on his neck and Jull countered with a swing of his large wing. He knocked the small moorhen completely over. Mik took the hit and rolled with it back to an upright position, but he wasn't ready to attack and

Jull was. The big muscovy brought his beak down with all his weight on Mik's shield. Again it knocked Mik down but not out. There was enough space between him and the muscovy commander for one hard blow. Mik took the chance and smashed Jull in the breast with everything he had left. At first, it appeared that the commander was only smiling at him; but he wasn't. He was beginning to sink. Mik was shocked. Then he remembered that muscovy had little oil in their feathers. Due to his own weight, Jull sank slowly underwater.

TWENTY SIX
AFTERMATH

Mik was still stunned when the last bubble of air from Jull's lungs broke the lake's surface. He quickly looked for his next challenger but none appeared. No bird was challenging any other bird. The war was over.

One would believe that cheering kuuuk's would pour from the beaks of the southern army, but that wasn't happening. Instead, the sound was deathly silence. The scene of devastation from the top of the Wide Bridge to the channel on the southern most end of the lake was overpowering. The distance as far as any birds eye could see was death and destruction.

When the surviving muscovy saw their commander drown, they knew it was inevitable that they would share the same fate and paddled to the nearest dry ground. Half of the northern army had been killed or disabled. Those too disabled to make it to land stoically accepted their fate as their waterlogged bodies slowly slipped beneath the beckoning lake. Those lucky enough to reach land were too wet to fly. Instead they began to walk. Although they didn't walk north; they walked west. Fear of the wrath of Greybeard kept them from believing they could ever return home.

Most of the anhinga survived, but gravely spread their wings to dry as they watched the muscovy sink or swim. The mottled ducks had made an early escape but returned to observe the carnage on their home lake. Bob and his ospreys only flew one pass over the ruined birds and needed to see no more. The few great white egrets that had joined the battle followed the osprey far off in the blue sky.

The limpkins and wood storks had received many losses, especially during the second attack on the bridge by the large numbers of viciously-trained muscovy commandos. Coal and Skrech had made it but both were limping from attacks on their legs and both were missing feathers. Both were also crying at the grave losses of their brothers and sisters.

The white-faced coots fared about as well as the moorhens. They accepted their loses and joined with their red-faced cousins in helping all wounded, no matter if they be southern or northern.

Mik looked first for Bek, but the mass of birds milling around the lake was tremendous. All the muscovy appeared to be trying to escape, some were helping others to the shore and some attempted to help injured birds where they floated. His heart was about to give up on Bek and allow himself to slip under the waves like so many others. He was just about to follow his thoughts when he heard the faint sound of a familiar kuuuk. He knew it had to be Bek's call and he bobbed madly in its direction.

After pushing through countless birds in all levels of physical condition, Mik finally found Bek. Both floated with necks entwined and wept without shame. When they finally kuuuked, Mik had to ask fearfully of Loug and his daughter. Both had seen the muscovy toss her about. Bek didn't know if she even survived. In the melee they had been separated. Together, Mik and Bek bobbed through the destruction surrounding them while kuuuking for their missing children.

The first child they found was Loug who was still hanging with Yaan. Yaan had lost a number of feathers but was otherwise unharmed. Loug seemed to be fine and continually bragged about all the muscovy he had smashed. Bek couldn't help but speak up to her son curtly. "You sound just like your father when he was young. Can't you see the awful destruction around you? And have you seen anything of your sister? We haven't been able to find her."

At his mother's chastisement, Loug could only hang his head in shame. He used the lowered head to shake, no. Then he looked up and countered eagerly. "We haven't seen her but we're happy to help find her. Right uncle Yaan?"

Yaan's voice sounded tired when he spoke. "Hold on, young moorhen. I'd love to help look for my niece but I'm all in and I have to check in on my own family. I have to head home now."

Mik and Bek understood Yaan's concerns and kuuuked him a goodbye for now and to kuuuk to Sheen for them. Yaan left and Mik, Bek and Loug continued the search.

They weren't long into their hunt before they saw a knot of white and red faces surrounding something. They all bobbed over to see what it was all about. When the group saw Mik they opened a path for him which led directly to his daughter. She was floating on her back with her wings spread out. Mik could see she was still breathing. Soon Bek shoved past Mik kuuuking the words, "My baby!"

Bek's baby was missing many feathers but when Bek asked her if she could move, she answered that she thought she could with a little more rest.

While his daughter rested, Mik looked at the wreckage around the lake. All the survivors of the war were moving toward their homes or helping those who, on their own, couldn't make the trip. He had lost many friends and enemies but in his reflections he realized there were no friends or enemies. All the birds and things in the world were connected as one. The sadness he felt was for everything, but he did know that with time the lake would naturally heal itself. As in the Battle of the Dark Marsh, the denizens of the lake, those feared creatures, would help clean up the mess.

When the injured daughter kuuuked she was rested enough to move, Mik and Bek turned her over. Loug managed to get each of her wings on both Mik and Bek's back and the family did a slow bob back to the Sanctuary.

TWENTY SEVEN
RETURN OF THE SAGE

For several days Mik didn't go out on the lake. He helped Bek nurse their daughter back to health. Loug had visited his other sister and had brought news that her brood was fine and her mate had made it through the war without injury. His world was turning back to normal until he heard a loud kuuuk coming from the reeds in front of the Sanctuary.

Mik left the nest to investigate but had little doubt about who he would find. It was of course, the Sage. He didn't know how to feel about his old friend and mentor. On one wing he felt that in its greatest time of need, the Sage had abandoned the lake. But on the other, the southern birds had beaten the northern army even with the blunders he had made as their commander. He thought yes, he was now considered the great hero, but he also didn't feel it made him any better than any other bird. At any rate, he had no choice but to kuuuk with the Sage and hear his excuse.

By the time Mik had reached the Sage his anger had won out and he kuuuked in fuming disrespect. "Where in the *Dark Marsh* have you been? While you were off gallivanting with your old friend we almost lost the entire lake. If it wasn't for Bob and the ospreys, and the egrets, we very well might have. Where have you been?"

The Sage understood Mik's anger and softened it by kuuuking, "I be not off gallivanting, whatever that may be. I be off burying my old friend. Doth that be alright with thee, *commander*?"

Mik's anger immediately turned to shame at how he had spoken to the Sage. "I'm so sorry. I had no idea you were on such a serious task. It must be terrible to hear me kuuuk as I did. I'm sorry."

"Don't be sorry Mik. I know you must have been feeling abandoned, but I be having no idea that the Ancient One be dying. Otherwise, I be not leaving thou in such dyer straights. But I be believing the minions of Greybeard be not invading a half moon cycle earlier than expected. He must have heard from his spy that I be gone."

Mik gasped at the word spy and kuuuked, "You believe there is a spy on the lake. How could that be?"

"Do not be so surprised, moorhen. I be knowing that thou hath seen strange goings on among the flock of ibis. As be I. We both be treated as ignorant fools by my treacherous cousin, Greybeard. But before my friend and mentor, the Ancient One, died he kuuuked me much about peculiar happenings on our lake. And before it be too late, our first duty must be to find this spy and find what he knows. If we do not, I be feeling my cousin hath much more damage tucked into his beard than he hath already caused.

And by the way Mik, so thou doth not feel so ill towards me, I must defend meself by kuuuking that I be asking Bob, the osprey, and the egrets to keep an eye on our lake while I be away."

Mik now remembered that Coal had told him about the osprey and egrets. The feeling of shame doubled, but before Mik could apologize for his lack of trust in the Sage again, the Sage reached his wing down on the moorhen's beak and kuuuked. "Say no more Mik. As I be teaching thou, what hath happened in the past be staying in the past. It is now. Our energies must be spent on finding our spy and be learning what he be knowing. You must be remembering what thou hath seen on the lake before I be leaving for the island of the Ancient One."

Mik put a wing to his head and strained to remember what he had seen. Then he kuuuked, "I remember a flock of ibis that for a long time stayed in one area. Usually they peck at the ground for a short time then move on. The only time I remember seeing this particular flock of ibis budge from the grassy knoll was when Bek and I mated and traveled to the Sanctuary. Soon after we moved, the same flock shifted close to the steep embankment across the channel. I never thought much about it until once when you and I kuuuked. Afterward, you flew off to the north to check on Greybeard. It was then that I noticed a deep grey-eyed ibis fly off after you. He was flying lower and faster than you, but I didn't give it much thought."

Usually the Sage didn't get excited but this time he did. "The grey-eyed one is the Ibis we be looking for. Is the flock still near the embankment?"

Before Mik could answer, Bek kuuuked from behind reeds where she had been listening. "They are still up there, wise one. I saw them this morning while I gathered food for my injured daughter. And another thing, the gossip on the lake is that no bird has seen Greybeard since before the war."

Both the Sage and Mik turned to the reeds in surprise until they heard Bek squeeze herself through the impediments and back towards the nest. Still excited, the Sage quickly kuuuked to Mik. "We be not having much time. We must be catching the grey-eyed one before he be flying his flock elsewhere. I be wanting thee to be staying here. Keep watch on the ibis but follow thy usual routine. We be not wanting him to get suspicious. In the meantime, I be going to find Coal and Skrech. We need more flying help, and we be needing it fast. Remember, if the ibis be flying off take note of their direction. I be sorry but for now there be not much more thee can do." Mick nodded in comprehension and the Sage spread his wings, and flew off to find Coal and Skrech.

As the Sage flew to where he had seen Coal before his trip to the island, he attempted to not look down. He didn't want to have to see the devastation which had occurred on the lake, but it was hard for him not to take a quick peek. He partly blamed himself for not being there for the war. When he did look, he saw that most of the destruction had been taken care of by the alligators and Ol' Mos. He was thankful for that but he remembered that until they were able to rid the lake of the *Black Menace*, nothing on the lake would be the same again.

When the Sage found Coal, he was forced to answer the same questions he had heard from Mik. He gave the same answers, including that they had a spy on the lake. Yes, he knew who it was and where he was presently. The Sage also wanted to know where to find Skrech as they needed his help. Coal told him that that would be easy as he and Skrech had become close war buddies since their combat on the Wide Bridge.

The Sage indicated that there wasn't much time to waste as the spy could leave at any time. Both took to the air and quickly found Skrech. The Sage gave the wood stork a quick explanation of where he had been and why they must fly immediately to the Sanctuary.

Mik was waiting by the reeds when the three large birds landed near him. He told them he hadn't seen much movement up near the embankment but had noticed the grey-eyed one occasionally look over the embankment. "I believe the Ancient One was correct. We've had a spy among us for awhile. Through her gossip network, Beck has learned his name is Zignoid."

Rashly, Skrech kuuuked first, "Let's get this Zignoid and pummel him until he kuuuk's what we need to know!"

The Sage hushed Skrech. There be no need for pummeling, Skrech. It be not Zignoid's fault. He be forced under a spell by Greybeard. What we be doing is capturing him and forcing him to tell his story. Maybe from there we can find my cousin and learn of a way to rid the lake of the Black Menace. We must be doing it now. If this Zignoid be seeing us together he may grow suspicious and fly off with his flock."

The Mik of old boldly kuuuked into the conversation, "I know what to do. I'll run up the hill and bash the daylights out of him. He won't fly anywhere then."

The Sage spoke up again. "There will be no bashing either, moorhen, and besides, thou will not be on this mission. I be not diminishing thee, but we need birds who can fly if he doth try to escape.

Now listen, this be the plan. Coal, Skrech and meself be flying slow and low over the embankment. When we reach the flock of ibis I will kuuuk loudly the name, Zignoid. He be bound to look up to find who be calling and when we see the grey eyes we all be surrounding him. If he be trying to flee, we grab his feet with our beaks. One of us be sure to stop him. Do thou all agree on this plan?" All heads nodded yes. "Then let us go."

The plan worked perfectly. The three largest birds slowly flew up over the embankment. Right before them stood the flock of ibis. The Sage kuuuked, *Zignoid*. He looked up. All three surrounded him. His deep grey eyes widened in fear and he stayed perfectly still.

TWENTY EIGHT
BLACK MENACE

When the three huge birds surrounded Zignoid, they found themselves encircled by Zignoid's flock, but all the large ibis flock did was to continue pecking at the ground for food. They were not birds who fought. Their only defense was a long bent beak used for eating. Their main defense was to walk or if real danger materialized, they flew away. For moments, the ibis flock merely pecked the ground they had already pecked over many moons and moved away from the embankment to a spot they had already pecked many moons before.

The Sage wasn't worried about the flock that surrounded the three large birds, but he waited until they had moved away before kuuuking to Zignoid. Then when he did kuuuk, he kuuuked in words Zignoid could understand. "Where be Greybeard?" The Sage could see the ibis was too frightened to speak and waved Coal and Skrech further away. "I ask thee again, Zignoid. Where be Greybeard?" Still no answer. The Sage tried again. "Do thou know where Greybeard be?"

This time Zignoid gave a one word nervous answer. "Yes."

"Then I be asking again grey-eyed ibis. Where be he?"

Zignoid was terrified of Greybeard but he also feared for his life now and answered. "He is on another lake."

"Why be he on another lake?"

The ibis was truly scared to answer that question. however, a greater fear of the three huge birds surrounding him triggered him to sputter out, "He's on another lake because he has eaten everything on the north end of this lake and the Black Menace ordered him to find another."

Tranquilly, as to not frighten the ibis any further, the Sage asked, "How do thou be knowing this, Zignoid?"

Zignoid thought about his answer for a long time and the other two large birds were running out of patience. Finally, he answered in a slow dribble of words. "I - know - because - I - know - everything - Black Menace - knows."

Hearing the answer, Coal, Skrech, and the Sage were all confounded. Though Coal kuuuked first. "How could you know what the Black Menace knows? It's on the other end of the lake. Are you kuuuking the truth or do we thrash it out of you?"

Now Zignoid was really terrified and it took all the Sage's composure to get him to speak again. "Please be telling us Zignoid. I be promising no harm be coming to thee. Now tell us, how could thou know what the Black Menace knows?"

To get the interrogation over with Zignoid blurted it straight out. "Greybeard put a spell on me. I am part of the Black Menace as are all the algae in its being."

The three birds were now confused, but Coal kuuuked. "How could that be possible? All birds know algae is but a single tiny creature. They've been in our lake since moons began."

Before the Sage could kuuuk, Skrech broke in. "If you know what the Black Menace knows, how did it find our lake? And be sure you kuuuk the truth."

Zignoid was shaken but angry. "I am telling the truth because I am the *Black Menace*. I came from a huge lake far to the west. I was once only a mass of separate blue green algae. But a terrible tempest blew up and my mass was struck by the flash of light from that storm. Suddenly, all the blue green algae in the mass turned black. Instead of us acting as many tiny creatures, we all thought and acted as one. Then a great blast of wind blew me from the overflowing lake into a steep channel of white water rapidly surging east. The journey I then traveled was terrible. Branches and rocks along the violent flow ripped at my whole body. My lower parts were shaved down to nothing by jagged gravel. I was falling to pieces. I felt myself shrinking as the swiftly flowing water pulled me through what seemed like a never ending nightmare of pain. Suddenly it stopped. I found what was left of me floating in the calm, marshy part of this lake.

It wasn't long before the shock of my change and new surroundings struck me. I knew not where I floated, but as shrunken as I had become, all of me was hungry. I began eating anything in the marsh I could absorb. In time even tiny fish were on the menu and I grew. The larger I grew the hungrier I became. Nevertheless, to move was impossible. My food supply dwindled. I had to find a way to eat.

One day a large silver fish swam close. I tried to absorb the big fish but it was too big. However, I did notice its color had turned from silver to deep grey. Not only had the color changed but I realized my thoughts could control its movements. It was like magic. Soon I had created a whole school of grey fish which swam around me, but it didn't solve my starvation. I would shrink again and maybe to nothing.

That's what I believed until a short while later when a large *great blue heron* came wading down the lake seeking a meal. I decided to give him one, a large grey fish. He ate it, fell unconscious and eventually woke. I quickly realized I could feel his thoughts and they were of hunger. I sent him more grey fish and realized my thoughts controlled him and his appetite fed me. We were unwitting partners."

The narrative of the *ibis/Black Menace* startled the Sage, but he still hadn't found the location of Greybeard. He was about to quiz the ibis about his cousin further when Mik came scamping up the hill next to the embankment.

Mik was kuuuking loudly about knowing how to make the Ibis talk. He rushed through the Sage's long legs, yanked a feather from the ibis' tail and swished it under his nostrils hoping the itch would force him to confess. "This will surely make him kuuuk." It didn't make him kuuuk.

It made him sneeze loudly. When he sneezed, a grey feather flew from his nostril, was picked up by a slight breeze, and blown out of sight. The ibis fell unconscious.

Quickly the Sage rushed to the lake, scooped a beak of water, came back to the ibis and dropped it on his face. The eyes of the ibis instantly popped open. They were now colored blue. When he scrutinized the gang leaning over him, Zignoid kuuuked, "Who are you?"

TWENTY NINE
ENDING THE MENACE

Anger flew at Mik from all the three large birds surrounding him until the Sage gained control of himself and calmed Coal and Skrech. Mik didn't understand why they were angry at him. It was Zignoid who was the spy. "Why are you all so mad at me? All I was doing was helping with the interrogation."

An exasperated wise Sage kuuuked first, "Mik, the Ancient One already be telling me the control Greybeard held over Zignoid be a feather jammed up his nostril. What be worse be that Zignoid be about to tell us the whereabouts of Greybeard. All we know now is that he be off ravishing another lake."

Mik held his head in shame and almost inaudibly kuuuked, "I'm sorry."

"Don't blame thyself Mik, thou be only trying to help." The Sage kuuuked, "besides, if Greybeard be not around we be having nothing to fear. The Black Menace cannot be moving about without his help."

After all the destruction to their flocks around the lake, Coal and Skrech were not ready to forgive Mik for his disastrous intrusion and flew off without a kuuuk.

Almost at once they were replaced by Bek who had come up to the hill beside the embankment to see what was going on.

The Sage noticed Bek and instantly kuuuked a greeting. When she came closer, he kuuuked the fact that he had heard her daughter had been hurt in the war and asked how she was faring. Almost out of breath from climbing the hill, Bek kuuuked that her daughter was coming along well. She felt her daughter would be back on the lake and inquired politely about the Sage.

When the pleasantries had been exchanged, Bek was introduced to Zignoid. When she heard the name she raised her wing to give him a bash, but the Sage held her wing back and explained how his spying had been Greybeard's fault. Bek took the Sage at his word, but she gave a glance to the ibis that was not friendly.

After seeing the look from Bek, the Sage felt he had better give Mik and Bek a complete narrative of how Zignoid became involved with Greybeard and the Black Menace. When he finished, the anger of both moorhens was soothed. However, they wanted to know if the Ancient One had given him any instructions of how to rid themselves of both Greybeard and the Black Menace.

The Sage shook his head with a no and kuuuked, "Before he died, the Ancient One described the feather in Zignoid's nostril but he be only saying that it be up to the three of us to figure out what to do next. That be one reason why I be happy thou hath joined us Bek."

Bek hadn't known about the death of the Ancient One and gave her condolences to the Sage. He thanked her for her kind words and kuuuked that the Ancient One had left this world happy and also kuuuked that he would explain his trip to the island at another time. Now they must put their heads together and figure a way to rid the lake of its most pressing two problems.

Mik spoke up quickly. "The Black Menace is pretty large and even if we could move it, where could we put it? It wouldn't fit under the Wide Bridge."

Bek broke in, "Even if we could move it, how would we keep ourselves from being contaminated? Look what Greybeard passed on to Zignoid."

The questions from the two moorhens began the Sage thinking. "If we be cutting it to pieces, we could be pushing it with long branches. However we not be knowing if touching the creature would harm us."

To their surprise it was Zignoid who spoke up next. "I do have a tiny bit of memory about what the Black Menace thinks while I was under its spell. I seem to remember it thinking that in the colder season its behavior changes. It doesn't need much food and it grows thinner. It might be that time that its power disappears and it could be broken into pieces."

"I be seeing what thou mean, Zignoid," the Sage kuuuked. "At the end of the Ancient One's life he kuuuked me a small clue. He be saying the Black Menace cannot live in water of salt. In the Great Sea I be tasting and smelling salt in that water. Nevertheless it be far from here."

Bek broke in, "If the Menace is chopped into small pieces we could push it to this sea of salt. It would die if what you are saying is true, wise Sage."

"If the Ancient One be saying it, it be true. But how could we break it up?"

Mik answered the Sage. "We have many birds on the lake with long sharp beaks. If we wait for the time between seasons we could chop it up and push it with branches to the place of the Salt Sea. I would do it for the lake and the future of my family."

Zignoid quickly spoke up. "This has always been the home of my flock. We move around much but always near this lake. Ibis have long beaks and I believe between seasons the Black Menace would pull itself tighter to preserve heat. It is then I believe the ibis' long beaks could break it up. Even if I were not conscious of it, I feel somewhat culpable for the Great War of the Wide Bridge. I know my flock would join me."

Bek kuuuked, "Wise Sage, you could kuuuk to Coal and Skrech and ask them and their flocks to scour the shore for long branches. All the swimming birds left on the lake understand we must be rid of the Black Menace in order to survive here. If we gather them all with branches we could push the Black Menace to the Salt Sea. Do you know how to reach it?"

A sudden memory of his beautiful Norce struck the Sage, but he was aware of the thought from the past and let it rest. He then nodded solemnly, yes. "I have traveled the channel by the Sanctuary, Bek. It leads to another lake with another channel that leads to the great Salt Sea. It could be done but it would be hard. I believe we be needing to take council with any birds on the lake who would join in such a venture."

Most of the birds on the lake who didn't migrate to other climates volunteered to join the *Cleansing of the Lake* as its legend was called.

When the time between seasons arrived, the plan was put into action. Zignoid had been correct; the Black Menace had tightened itself and all his flock took part in chopping it up after a warning from the Sage not to swallow any of the algae. Greybeard did not interrupt nor had he been seen since the war.

Once the Black Menace had been chopped to pieces, the Sage and the others watched the ibis for any signs of contamination; there were none. It was then decided to leave the branches behind. After a warning from the Sage to watch out for alligators, the swimming birds, including Mik and Bek, followed the Sage and each pushed small pieces of the Black Menace all the way to the Sea of Salt. It was a long journey and by the time they all returned, a new season had started. Mik and Bek were happy and were soon due for another brood.

THIRTY
ANOTHER SEASON

The trip to the Salt Sea had been horrendous. The current had helped leading to it, but the birds on the journey had to stop for food, rest and sleep. A few of the birds lost their lives to alligators and turtles. Nevertheless other birds managed to control an extra piece of the Black Menace. After traveling down three channels and crossing two lakes, they all breathed a sigh of relief as they watched the black scourge pulled out to sea on the ebbing tide.

Any of the birds who skipped migration to help rid the lake of its Menace, such as some mottled ducks and white-faced coots flew home. However, the contingent of moorhens had no choice but to battle the channel flow back to their lake; that included Mik and Bek.

When Mik and Bek finally saw the stand of bamboo which was their Sanctuary, they rushed through the reeds hiding their nest and rested until hunger drove them for food. In a few spring moons they were happy and frisky. It wasn't long before Bek laid another brood and in twenty moons they hatched three eggs. Both moorhens were disappointed at having only three hatchlings. It was a small amount but they blamed it on the arduous journey they had recently taken.

Both birds still took their turn incubating their eggs, and both birds still meditated as they did. Turning to their knowledge of mindfulness, Mik and Bek soon changed their minds from disappointment to joy at having produced three healthy hatchlings. It wasn't long before the hatchlings grew to fledglings and Mik and Bek began taking them across the channel for their training to maturity.

Unfortunately, this brood didn't fare as well as most of their earlier families. On the day they had just introduced their fledglings to the Sage near the flat shore, there was a major mishap on the channel as they headed back to the Sanctuary. The last fledgling in the line following their parents was abruptly pulled beneath the water, not to rise again. Quickly the rest of the family rushed through the reeds to their nest and all four moorhens wept for their loss.

It was only a few moons later when the family was pushing through the reeds to the channel that the large, open white mouth of a water moccasin seized the last fledgling in line and dragged him away to his death. The wildness of the lake had taken another victim.

Mik and Bek now had only one fledgling to train and they agreed to protect it with their lives. They didn't travel the channel without the little one between them and the fledgling was never left alone. Still, the way of nature cannot always be forced to cooperate.

One day they were across the channel teaching their lone fledgling to eat from the bottom of the lake when the sky turned black. Mik suggested they all make a fast bob back to the Sanctuary. They were halfway across the channel when the clouds released a horrifically windy rain storm. The three birds bobbed furiously for the Sanctuary. Sadly the slight weight of the young fledgling couldn't hold him down. An appalling gust of fierce rain-filled wind pulled him out of the water and into the black sky.

Mik and Bek made it to the Sanctuary and anxiously waited for the end of the quick moving squall. They then scoured the channel and lake, calling for their last fledgling until the sun was high in the sky. It was to no avail. Finally giving up, they met in the center of the channel, touched their red beaks, and held their grief stricken selves neck to neck.

When the Sage heard about Mik and Bek's tragedy, he immediately flew to the Sanctuary and he helped them meditate through their grief.

By the time it reached mid-season, Bek had produced another brood of six eggs. Both moorhens were happy to sit and meditate on their new future family until they had hatched. At the time of their hatching both Mik and Bek swore they would let nothing stop them from raising their six hatchlings to mature moorhens.

They were happy with their family and kept a close watch over them through the course of their early lives. Finally, it was time to take them for their first trip out on the open lake. The hatchlings were feeding under-water near the flat shore across the channel when Mik gave them the news. They would all be taken out to the open lake for the first time.

The fledglings were excited and kuuuked that they wanted to leave then. Mik and Bek couldn't refuse their anxiety ridden-excitement.

Mik left the shore first, followed by Bek, and then came the straight line of six excited fledglings. They left the shoreline where the hill started and the embankment began. They had just bobbed to the center of the high, flat embankment across the channel from the Sanctuary when a streak of blue flashed past Mik. The blue flash landed a wing's length out in the channel, looking into Mik's eyes. It was Greybeard.

Mik had no time to think. Nevertheless, a natural sense to protect his family led him to instantly lower his head and bash into Greybeard's gut. The great blue heron was knocked back two steps, but only laughed. The wallop did give Bek enough time to gather all the fledglings behind her. Then, they tried to blend in with the flat wall of dirt and weeds making up the embankment.

When Greybeard stopped laughing, he kuuuked at Mik and Bek, "Why do you bother even trying to hide your tiny fledglings? Nothing can stop me from devouring all the little snacks. And both of you shall be my desert."

Mik and Bek looked into each other's eyes. No kuuuk was heard. Only a silent agreement passed between them. It stated; nothing will hurt our family.

Mik was the first to act. He smashed Greybeard in the gut again. He only had time to move backward when Bek smashed him head down again. By now Mik was ready and Greybeard was hit again, then by Bek, by Mik, by Bek, Mik, Bek, Mik, and Bek. Greybeard's eyes rolled up in his head and he fell against the embankment.

Before Greybeard could slide into the water, a whoosh of white wings landed the Sage next to the exhausted moorhens. When Mik finally caught his breath, he kuuuked to the Sage, "How did you know he was here?"

The Sage was looking at Greybeard but kuuuked to Mik, "I be seeing him crossing the lake and guessed where he be going. I be correct."

Bek kuuuked, "Is he dead? I hope he is dead. He was about to devour our fledglings along with us. I hope he's dead."

"No, no, Bek, but thou be knocking the stuffing out of him."

Bek kept on, "He should be dead. Dunk his head underwater and finish him off. To the lake he has done so much terrible damage."

Mik quickly agreed with Bek but the Sage had a better idea.

"Listen to me moorhens. You be hearing the tale of Zignoid. Thou be knowing Greybeard be not all to blame. I be thinking of a better place than in the *nothing*."

Mik kuuuked, "Then what shall we do?"

The Sage kuuuked quickly, "First, I be wanting Bek to take her fledglings back across the channel to the Sanctuary. Then, I be flying to gather some friends to help. And thee Mik, I be wanting thou to stay with Greybeard. If he be coming conscious I want thou to hit him again until he be not. Be thee understanding?"

"I'll smash him all you want."

The Sage kuuuked a laugh and flew off. He returned soon leading three great white egrets. Greybeard was still unconscious and the Sage didn't waste any time. He asked two of the egrets to use their beaks to drag Greybeard over to the flat shore past the embankment. Then he asked the other egret to claw a deep hole in the soft sand a distance from the water. They all took on their tasks without a kuuuk.

Soon, Greybeard was on his back next to the deep hole and the Sage asked the first two egrets to stand on Greybeard's wings but to be careful not to hurt him. Mik watched the procedure in silence as the Sage began plucking the grey feathers from his cousin's chest. Each feather he pulled, the Sage dropped carefully into the hole. When he was sure every grey feather was removed, he asked the third egret to claw the sand back into the hole to bury the feathers.

As the Sage walked to the channel for water to wake Greybeard, Mik couldn't help but ask, "What will happen to Greybeard now wise Sage? You can't just let him go."

The Sage kuuuked the answer as if he had always known what he would do. "I be taking him to the island of the Ancient One. The three egrets will be accompanying in case there be trouble."

Horrified, Mik asked, "Won't he use his natural senses to find his way home?"

"No little moorhen. The island be far off out in the Salt Sea and we be taking a roundabout route. He be lost at sea and be never bothering us again."

Mik quickly bobbed across the channel to tell Bek the plan for Greybeard. They both left the Sanctuary and watched the Sage, his cousin, Greybeard and the three egret guards fly away. They watched until they could only see five specks in the sky.

When the specks completely disappeared, Mik turned to his mate and kuuuked, "Soon we'll have the fledglings out on the lake and soon after they will be grown to maturity, Beck."

Bek kuuuked, "You are correct, Mik. But soon after that, the cycle will begin again. She then nipped him on the neck.

EPILOGUE

Greybeard stood at the edge of the pool and watched the fish swim in circles. The circles reminded him of the route his cousin and the three egrets had taken to lead him to this lonely island. He'd tried everything to find his way back to his home lake but whatever direction he flew in he could find nothing but blue sea.

He no longer felt insatiable hunger. Nevertheless, he found himself spearing a fish for the sake of feeling it wriggling down his gullet. When the feeling ended, he wondered again who had built the small dam that held back some of the water which collected his food.

Not all the water stayed in the pool, some of it ran over the top of the dam through a short stretch of jungle and across the beach. It then emptied into a tidal pool by the sea.

If Greybeard knew the term *brackish*, the mixture of salt and fresh water, he would have paid more attention. As he speared another fish, he didn't think about the tidal pool or about the small wave which into it, pushed a minute piece of *black algae*.

www.ingramcontent.com/pod-product-compliance
Lightning Source LLC
LaVergne TN
LVHW011936070526
838202LV00054B/4673